MW01689720

Mold Sustaining

Antoni Fares

with:

So You May Hold the Sun in Your Hands—
A Brief First Installment of a Trilogy

PublishAmerica
Baltimore

First printing

At the specific preference of the author, PublishAmerica allowed this work to remain exactly as the author intended, verbatim, without editorial input.

ISBN: 1-4137-3432-4
PUBLISHED BY PUBLISHAMERICA, LLLP
www.publishamerica.com
Baltimore

Printed in the United States of America

In efforts to resurrect
the walking dead

Derrick
i know we don't have
much more than a
client-patron association
but it's good to know you
& i thoroughly enjoy our
happenstance conversations
underground. thanks for your
support
Antoni farer

*This malnourished body of prose is Dedicated to you—**Mac spACEy**.*

*This is where I stroke your ego; where I recognize the value of your shrewdness. You know I always look to you for acceptance. **Mac spACEy** facilitates & increases my sight, speech, and radical epistemology. It is my pleasure then to nod the reciprocating nod and knock fists for the Dartain squad.*

Mark Ryken

Without the countless hours you donated I would be scarcely able to bring a project worthy of distribution to fruition. Fuck man, you worked on the patriot missile. I know you don't need to be rendering low resolution pictures of the not always so photogenic me presentable, to get your 3 minutes of celebreality. Thank you for aiding to make the release of my debut work actual. I intend to never forget it.

05/06/01
self-trait

you feel empty maybe
full in the head
but empty in the soul
lacking will for life

It's bewildering how crippling conditions become customary.
It's so easy to hate and wade in the shallow end all your live-long life.

By the way…

* * First Impression * *

The apartment complex abounds with grouped units of crowded, compartment stature. This disturbs the reclusive male specimen; a fairly new tenant and first time renter of no consequence. He is merely one of several hundred inhabitants, all of a similar status and pedigree in limited respects.

Every edifice is painted marine-green. The trim and the door are a deeper shade, more steeped in blue. Above, a densely forested canopy inundates and is an eyesore for its monotony. The extensive networks of leaf-littered branches which tower some thirty feet overhead almost never sway in this stale, central valley climate.

Deep (as in deep, deep) blue-green door...two-two-four...*the numbers*...you know.

Beyond this entrance, a docent showcases. It is the specter of the specimen. A holographic narrator employed to interject dispassionate commentary; a *pro bono* PR Shade, if you will.

Be not alarmed, it implores. Tread intrusively. Scan his sanctuary. Violate him! Arouse him!

It is not breaking and entering if there's no sign of forced entry.

Ask, "Where is he?"(This Shade expects curiosity on your part)

Well, if you must know he is preoccupied with justifying defensively. He's concentrating. That's his whole point & sole purpose and he needs to quit it! Actually he's homeward bound via antique single-speed.

"His existence?"

Bravo! That's a mighty good question.

Now...one word for his existence: pessimistic. He's a young cynic in suburbia where there is inadequate stimulus and more shelter than he can bear. With him the glass is not half full. There is no glass. Many times daily he's reminded of the insurmountable futility of conceiving the man of his dreams. He sells himself short because he doesn't realize God bestows value.

He's told people what they do isn't inspiring, then cared about them. He's slandered & backbitten players he ought to regard as fellows avenging perceived airs of disapproval & hostility. Consequently he's assumed the nickname 'The Dissident'. He's the 32nd flavor apparently. Not long ago, he actually went up on stage at an open mic under the aforementioned alias. In this den he was dissed by inebriated/ *spirited peeps*. He was dissed and subsequently quit, feeling like languid shit for being a poet. That he night he dreamt of farming Christmas trees. His intuition told him he merely longed to mow, already sparse forests down with a chainsaw.

That's just the way it is. He is very serious today; not down for an afternoon cruise through the boonies. He might smoke bong loads for 52 weeks or behave like five year old fed LSD by his hippie, communal-living quote, unquote *parents*—less violent perhaps, more psychotic. Besides he had an '88 Accord—when there was a car leased. It was a fucking pile. The clutch went to the floor on his way to Vegas on a whim after midnight with some friends and didn't come back. They spent all their funds to tow it back from the last Fresno exit, just across the Clovis city limits, by an operator who claimed to tow Michael Jordan every time he was in town, who was always delighted to shoot hoops with his six-year-old: true story.

Speaking of addresses, UNTIL FURTHER NOTICE This Dissidents prefers to be addressed as This Mister—that's This Mister, not T.M., Misled or Misfit. This Mister is overtly introverted & several people probably consider him a fucking airhead who only knows how to hurt people.

This Mister believes he can bicker forever, avoid confrontation at all costs, and refuse to substantiate the sources of his misery. The source of his misery is uncertainty. That's not an answer. Surely you're well aware.

Oddly enough This Mister really can be as serene as basket weaving. Unfortunately he has fit much distance between defected confidants and himself. These days he accomplishes pitifully little in the way of maintaining contacts, acquainting with new folks, or hosting company. He imitates the archetype of celebrated writers of yesteryears. However, Fresno doesn't even know where he's from. Nevertheless it helps him feel relevant to feign guilt for neglecting such would-be duties.

A squanderer of youth; he's resigned himself, as an elder teen, to frequenting his workplace, his dwelling, & the grocery store exclusively.

* * Prologue * *

At the same time he is desperate to write the terms of his reception to anybody, seeing as he has no person to vent his mounting frustration. He has argued intemperately, trivialized, and vented scorn; indicating discontent precisely. These methods of engaging have proven disastrous. He has not gained any remarkable notice by his outbursts. He's been friends latered; ruining the molested hours of his own days, only. Anger has disturbed this water now: stagnant, muddy, & contaminated.

The immediate shock ripples of This Mister's pleas have passed. He is no longer news.

What is he to do?

This Mister is a studious hysteric. He can't cope with much less negotiate the complexity of his feelings. However he concedes: some universal order must have been asserted by a grand architect at the inception. Otherwise he'd find it impossible not to buckle, weak in the knees before universal chaos, to be smitten by infinite styles of oppressive mockery. A revelation of Divine Justice would be a Godsend. (Not to be confused with gospel).

Nevertheless This Mister is without the capacity to fear God. Instead he toys with numerology. This is all intellectual babbling. As far as This Mister is concerned Divine Redemption is the ultimate incentive. He fancies how he may direct his endeavors through to fulfillment thereof; operating just as he exerts force to quietly close a door so not to disturb napping inhabitant's afternoon delight. This does not mean he's a success executing. This Mister has had the: Hindrances Are Discouraging life lesson drilled into his cranium about a dozen times. This Mister used to be an expectant adolescent. He's hardly a legal adult—"So what though?"

The setting and philosophy

Once grown, one's dreams aren't supposed to intimidate, frighten and paralyze any longer. An Adult rises to get on with their day. An Adult blitzes the morning. An Adult has Promotion on the run. An Adult regards less Enigmatic Dreams.

This Mister loathes his dependence on the Material Realm & is ashamed to be defined the excuses he's invented to flee responsibility. He's adapted without strategy; the essence of despair. Now everyday feels like a compromise. He feels powerless. He thinks we all are, that we are all supplanted by false dilemmas—*shows what he knows.*

On with the tour of his dwelling...

This Mister's dwelling resembles a ½ gallon milk carton—except the roof is lean-to rather than A-frame—and there's not a huge placard entitled HAVE YOU SEEN ME? on one face. Hefty lumber ascends from the top of the façade to the rear of the building. The head of this ray is some twenty plus feet in the rear. The loft area is fenced along the overhang and beside the stairwell.

Shrouded exclusively in a distant lighthouse, the subject at home intends to manipulate shadows and metaphors on his own terms to render an original composition. He is not serving seafarers, landlocked as he is.

This Mister's townhouse style loft apartment is certainly

not opulent, nor is it especially spacious. There is a psychedelic peace sheet tacked to the south wall on the ground level. It's tie-dye, a high school Honors Chemistry project. It's pretty large, the size of a twin bed sheet A huge magenta peace sign is in the foreground before a dye spill: sky blue, pale yellow, and tangerine with hints of pink bleeding from the ☮

Beyond the living room is the kitchen; its components tucked behind a partition. In the corner this partition meets another partition that encloses the staircase. These partitions are the inner West & North walls, respectively. A dwarfish closet door provides access to the hollow area beneath the stairs. The space is an interesting selling point: *great potential for a grow room*. The complex management likes to joke with the appropriate suspects. The staircase runs along the east side of the building. They are right before the entryway; set up to bound upon, or slide down on cardboard sleds, into mattresses and occasionally wildly into the front door.

The lean-to ceiling rests in the rear on an oblong & stubby white-wonder-wall. Every night This Mister lay in the mouth of the ascending ray, staring to find sleep. Without necessarily fixing his eyes on anything this textured & breathing wall entrances. He buys into the illusion of its depth and tunes into the hallucinogenic evening program. Then he passes on into recuperating for the next morning.

If in interpreting dreams we can more consciously be, we ought to record them primarily, or devote more time to developing the art of daydreaming into the practice of thought-experimentation. This Mister jolts up shocked and trembling often in the still of night, where only locusts and rare savages thrive. He avoids remembering.

There are two doors interrupting the sheer magnificence of the wide & stout slab. The door on the left is the closet and it is closed. His clothing is light but can conquest through. The other door to the bathroom is open atop of the staircase.

The underlay of the apartment is where all the action matters. There is a certain art to living. There will be evidence of every human instance no matter what. But what permits us to thrive? What is the recipe of life? We have to wake up into our own skin-suit and arise. Unless something goes terribly wrong we conduct in pursuit of destiny, *or do we just grind on the daily?* Having the courage to face our fears propels us into future predicaments. A human's essential self-conflict is a human's struggle for integrity is a human's reason for being. In negotiating this predicament a being is established and authenticated.

One can look over the banister and spy on forms in the stairwell or entry. Espies can peer over the hunched back of the composing, if they be diligently drafting at the table in the SE corner. The blinds are drawn before the two panes: one stationary, one sliding glass pane in the east wall. Although the sun rises to bless this room, the concaved file of plastic blinds swaying slightly, always in pendulum decay, shuts out the light.

This Mister: a candidate for the prince of rejection fails at being sympathetic and is terribly poetic. He may complicate your faith, which is reprehensible. He will go out an amateur; a drained lover, marveling at issues aroused. Such as: we have to train our eye to see beauty? Condition our mind to recognize the beautiful & splendorous? Thought is required to be carried away in a painting?

If one looked up from the outskirts of the room and tried to look up through the banister to the sleeping realm, it would be difficult to see due to broken halves of battered decks strung by wire through their hardware holes. These mobiles dangle blocking the open slots in the banister between the posts.

There are no other windows or other openings other than the two panes beside the front door opening out to the fenced patio. Outside there are a multitude of projects in gestation.

Nostalgia can be decent. If you don't stubbornly stay, even when it's apparent how unwelcome you are. Distractions sustain temporarily. People who aren't grateful for their status, their niche, their cliché, or for what they've achieved, people who feel defeated, people who don't bother to raise concern, people who'd rather respond with a grimace, people who don't confront, feel awkward belonging. They are most often a mystery, inaccessible, aloof. They retreat into the past or, if lucky might flip on naivety briefly, before they are blown by reality. They are predisposed to turning off, which might be considered extreme daydreaming.

Compulsive disengagement is not healthy. Relationships turn like spoiled sardines in mustard grease when an internal monologue dominates, and no substance is imparted amongst/between engaging parties.

This Mister on the renter's agreement is on his way home, from the grocery store.

The outside property is surrounded by fences and holds strange objects, scattered yet somewhat arranged—a few ordered. In the outside world the majority sustain the clichés.

They are no tamer then he: baboons befouling, scrambling to privatize indiscretions. The powerless are nameless, are exasperated, hopelessly defending with remarks like, "It's just me" pitifully parting the crowd; inertia consumed by non-conservative forces.

Presently on his way to solitary detention, This Mister doesn't know why, he must polarize himself. Possibly it's the way the days work him into grinding his teeth—his fucking teeth...

Is there truly a unique soul upon this Earth? Or do we act special, when we can't be original? Do we seem ugly for aspiring? The vanity of composure is deplorable even though—the melodramatic are fond of whispering "I like me" exuberantly in seldom occurring overwhelming fits of giddiness.

There are so many appropriate classifications plaguing the indecisive adolescent who cannot substantiate a mature (guardian male) air. His tendency to react is primarily a character flaw. He makes the excuse: when you get too deep into yourself, it's hard to fight anything, to understand or even accept your feelings. Depression is never counteracted with excessive lifestyles. The depressed never seem able to practice moderation. Should everyone have an analyst? Why don't they come in a box? Damn it! Why aren't they marketed commercially? Why isn't there a solution capitalizing? A capsule form? Analysts are to Narcotics as Artists are to heaps of Stegosaurus shit…*or something…*

It can't be possible to worry all the time. Wrong! There are hoards of delusional, pessimistic, incessant, paranoid, worried, worn people in the world that lock themselves in role playing games in the mind that involved situations that are unrealistic and usually devastating to themselves, because they are delusional, pessimistic, incessant, paranoid, worried and worn people who are locked in role playing conquests. They don't do much but rape this over-abundance of quality time in confinement.

The length of fence perpendicular to the building has a gate that opens, permitting admittance through to possibly flee through the open gateway out to the community of dense natural foliage where there are leaves, and needles, the aqua green buildings, the forest green doors and siding and the avocado green fence stakes.

Escape provides emergency relief for nervous tension. Whimsical and counterproductive; coping somehow. Who's to talk in a negative descent about another's sense of relief? Is business open throughout? Free exchange throughout? This Mister's streaming conscious keeps him company as he cycles homeward.

On the other side of the fence is the inward opening front door with the dull brass numerical markers, *remember?* Ironic or appropriate: they are? *–his unit number*

Enlightenment is gradually occurring. It comes from everything. It is a radiating pulsating energy ball which ricochets from surface to sport to novel to love to theft to jail to journey to life & all through life this energy ball collects mass. Through your whole life your manners will evolve as you discover tranquility, or become impossibly frustrated and inevitably enraged, or cheated from your destiny, or some other series of tragedies shall befall you, because you probably won't be happy.

Life and experience is rarely received openly. Who wants to hear, much less take something of what is on another's mind? Too self-absorbed to care, people just want to be entertained. And he is not the furthest from collectivism. What he knows of the Orient & the spirit, he dines with. For dessert: overtly fatal beliefs and natural gas probably.

No one can really appreciate art; for it is the token of a mind. This is for the best as well, as artists are unusually full of shit. They are arrangers of splendorous colored portrayals. They are imaginative designers, and formulators of context when they ought to be water to flush pretension.

They, artists, ought to usher and then exit. Adieu, parting is *such a relief* Shakespeare—some Earth-goddess you courted there and everywhere, you're stalking dream deities! For goodness or the sake of...*SUSPEND!*...You are so aggravating! Such bourgie-wannabes!

The stairs to eternity are illuminated upon the completed arc of the door. A small lamp is posted on the wall near the top of the flight for the safe scaling of this steep and trip-worthy case. Patience is a priceless virtue. While waiting, stragglers linger like a bitter burn in the trachea.

How easy it is to daydream, and virtually project the course of events in the future. Dull, certainly as passages of life are. Six months of the average human being's lifespan are spent at red lights. Do you need 2/3 more of your life to devote to sleep?

The anxiety is maddening at times, especially for those who wish quantum leap to another decade, another contemporary society. Memories are corruptible and guarded; revealed only if confident of company.

Permissiveness is forgetting you have to wait for anything and pretending you have everything. Rarely can we be well and need nothing. At times This Mister has felt like a transient and was able to disregard the time factor: his nemesis. A vagabond treks to forget time must be kept; leaving the pocket watch and wallet behind on the desk of his/her cubicle.

In the main This Mister is squandering his youth on his subscription to fatalism. He uses pretension as a defense mechanism. Since there is no tomorrow his concern is for self primarily.

He's living, for the time being.

"I need to do something nice for a wretched organism," he mutters under his breath as he fiddles with is keys.

The case of stairs is the primary source of memory. Memories diffuse from this base area over somewhat lively nights when eminently pulsating hysterics forced life to reveal all its gruesome truth as well as its natural splendor to those eating strips of perforated cardstock. Imagine this is actually enjoyable; that senses, especially sight, become ever so acute—and not just the optical sensibility entrusted to eyes but also the mind's perceptive faculties which read body language, subtle nuances, and vibes.

Id is available for conversation. The impulsive bestial projection repressed conscientiously can sensually be instigated and will aggressively motivate towards some irresistible end when this end is magnetically attractive enough. Id is rather easily aroused—it might surprise some. And though Id is immaterial Id is quite eager matter of fact, to be invigorated by the deliberate ego daring enough to insist Hyde step out to feast. Id will oblige. Id will abominate. Id will reign. Id will terrorize geese, and strip sheep of their fleece.

Id is not concerned with the consequences of any dastardly rampages. Never has Id wielded enough influence to contrive. Id doesn't know Hyde's alive, is reviled, is unbridled, Id cannot reckon or decide, cannot recognize he's even engaged in libel. Hyde propels from Id, acting on the fly.

Id is genuinely mean. Id genuinely means to expel the rawest Hyde.

Fleeing passionately from confinement: Id is civil only when coincidentally considered appropriate, for Hyde doesn't know Id from Aristotle and Id doesn't know what appropriate is much less how to be a beast though Hyde does so spectacularly well it's ironical.

* * 2 * *

The door opens. With a great intensity of light penetrating around him through the doorway a man finds entrance. He has tanned apricot skin and appears to be carrying groceries. He sets a plastic bag against the slender strip of wall between the front door and the sliding glass panel. As he drops his left arm flakes of orange rind flutter to the carpet and some land in the small tiled area of the entryway.

He exits and returns carrying a late-model Schwinn single speed. He carries it in backwards and walks the bike back so the rear tire is under the drafting table in the corner then leans the bike gently against the blinds.

This Mister is clad in beige cutoffs and gray Tee with gradating florescent picture of pines in the foothills striped across his chest. The filter gradates magenta-yellow-tangerine left to right. In block letters below, the word CHA_WAN_A_KEE is stamped in capitals with the same color scheme. He's a five-year patron of this BSA scout camp; a Sachem by their standards, of the tribe of Chawanakee who once thrived in the Shaver Lake Area before the white man erected his dam. Incidentally, the first two failed, much to the pleasure of the guardian spirits of the forest and its native inhabitants. This Mister was part of the most dysfunctional troop. They could band together to accomplish feats but there was no real or enforced regimentation. It was casual, about the experimental traversing of limits.

A foreign skin overcomes for he is of Lebanese descent. His dear, departed father ventured to the bloody red heart of Los Angeles to study medicine at its U.C. from the shrieking cedars felled in Lebanon to escape serious sectarian warfare circa '68.

His hair, eyes, and thin beard are all medium brown. A mass of wooly hair is tied into dreads behind and between the ears. The hair atop his head drapes concealing the beaver tails and the sinuous clubs which flank it. Tying up the underlying hair allows for the over layer of his helmet to fall along his facial structure rather than protrude out as an anthill to his shoulders.

He slings his backpack around his right shoulder and flings it atop the drafting table. He doesn't intend to leave the orange peels as litter. Kneeling to retrieve he recalls how their taste is the sweetest of sweets. This Mister assigns a symbolic meaning to the orange: it represents love: the endearment. Love he's admonished, nay banished: the love of man; the cherisher of God, of woman. This mister swallows, nay gulps; sorrowfully rebuked. There's one word, but don't utter—

He bends over to pickup the pieces.

Sliding the glass barrier aside, one piece of the peel tumbles swiftly down. He bends to pick it up pushing his gluteus back. An ovular patch with flat bottom of the Lebanese flag within a yellow border is sewn over a tear on the right check of his short pants. The banner consists of two red stripes, top & bottom surrounding a white middle ground with the appropriate cedar (for the Americans). He turns to the right alongside the glass surface.

He walks around an exiled end table with paint all over it and the words 'EAT ME' marked on the tabletop. Atop, a petite black charcoal barbeque hull is loaded and standing by.

The orange peels are dropped into a fish tank that keeps the mulch pile he grows in bounds. Its present status is marshy, emitting a putrid smell. Several souring oranges, resting fruitfully cloud the senses in the swampy course. A foldable camping spade is staked into this mound of mud potato peels, apple cores, head of lettuce, muck of tomato, celery stalks and the illustrious oranges. He cinches the blade into place, wrenching the handy locking nut.

He poses the spade and lunges, stabbing at the oranges maliciously with contempt for his wanton state, and intolerable longing for companionship. His lance crooks and his forces are hampered. The spade had begun to waver after several thrusts piercing the thin rinds exposing mushy orange flesh. He finds he's unearthed a disgusting dust. He coughs with the contrived repugnance of one exclaiming just after uttering some tactless and cliché phrase of inflated pain.

A break in his hostile intent, he suddenly pauses, but only to wrench the nut further. He then takes his position, readies, jukes and lunges several times more, mutilating the cores in furious silence. He then turns the mud, heaving it upon the oranges and slapping them back-handed with the spade. Then swinging the shovel in a pendulum motion below his waist he slams an edge into the aquarium. This blow cracks but does not shatter the glass. He does not appreciate the extent of his own dismay. It is at this point that he drops the spade beside him and returns within the confines of his den, sealing himself in.

He is next enticed enough by the grocery bag in the corner. He transports it into the kitchen by a table at his left, tangent to the wall. Four olive green comfy leather padded chairs are crowded around a lousy three hundred degrees. Green may be some people's favorite color. They: the table & chairs were free—not people's choice of a favorite color. Don't get it twisted.

He sets the bag on a slender countertop beside the stove top. As sure and quick as he dipped for the towel paper roll the night has begun. Though he's still with and in the sweat of four:thirty in the afternoon roasting This Mister now stepping off of calamity avenue into the abyss of his dwelling.

Right and left wing to the stove are twenty inch wide counter tops. Left wing is where all the fruits are kept: lemons, oranges, many oranges—because they pain immensely yet are so scrumptious. A large grapefruit holds it down and now two green apples are removed from the grocery bag. The fruits aside the new additions all bear names:

Meet the oranges: Paul, Jean, Stephan, Maurice, and Mel Gibson.

Meet the lemons: Guinevere, Elsa, Citrus, and Ayisha.

Meet Arnie: the grapefruit.

Arnie, the real flesh, is separate from the others, atop a throw towel's pad. Arnie reckons itself cast from the testosterone imbued flesh orange. Arnie's filters exacerbate the restrictive demeanor of the jovial yellow citrus in succulently supplanting. This berates his charisma as well. Arnie reminds This Mister of someone he knows. Someone seeking ownership on his reservations for no like kind confirms with enough encouragement to wrestle numbness from the cotton tuft grown before it's industriously picked by *the gin*.

A jar of bay leaves is removed and set on the ledge above the oven controls. At the end of the corridor is his fridge and across, on the inner side of the partition is a shallow pantry. He carefully leans the package of cumin on a shelf eye level—two noticeable bobs of the head for the cumin's absurdly bestowed celebrity status. The bag reminds him for some odd reason of Marlon Brando & the Streetcar bravado.

With an imagination that runs wild, even a sober mind is out alone on the tiles.

Lastly, he puts a frozen can of concentrate in the freezer door and applies implosive force to the empty plastic bag several times. The snap of the force evacuating all air persists as he wrinkles into a ball shoots it underarm into the cupboard beneath the sink; slamming the door back into place. A quick gallop back over to the desk to open the larger compartment of his back agent. He pulls out a can of corn, a can of garbanzo beans, two yellow onions in a bag, a red and green pepper with the onions, a small bunch of mint leaves, three Roma's, an otherwise ordinary tomato. And of course a red party light bulb—although he can't hold onto it. It slips out his hands and tumbles off the side of the desk. He retrieves it and moseys back to the kitchen, tossing it onto the kitchen table in its cardboard container and he bumps into the chair trying to get by. Fortunately the bulb does not break even though it's been terribly rattled.

He places his load of vegetables and cans on the countertop left wing to the sink where boneless chicken thighs on a plate have been defrosting since the morn. He stacks the cans, corn over the bean the top one leaning over a bit. He reaches through the wavering plastic sack and pulls out the green bell pepper and tosses it into the prepared bath, its hollowness and thin walled layer leaves an almost undisturbed pool as it lands right on top of the surface seemingly. The much longer red pepper shoots up a substantial streak of liquid which falls in individual beads when it collides with the film surface of the pool.

He allows mint leaves in his hand to flutter down with no doubt, a measure of infidelity. They catch a decent rest, like lily pads in a reflecting pond, giving of an aroma fine and profound. He obtains a bunch of parsley from the crisper compartment in the fridge and tosses it over his back. Then he pulls out strings of green onion; one and two, deciding against a third. This area he's working upon is especially long; elongated because it is the only wing of the sink. The sink's right wing is but a nub, butted against the outer wall of the pantry.

There is a bowl of soaking lentils presently in the unused inlet of that sink. He reaches inside the wavering bag for the Roma's: VIPs at this Roman bath session. Three of the slim & fittest Roma soldiers are respectfully eased into the bath to soothe and soak their thin skin and invertebrate composition.

Next the king: just a plump version of the same specie? No—but he's too vain to admit alien specie. He did not rise through the phalanx to the commander of legions. He did not litigate in the senate yet his Praetorian guard has pledged allegiance. Alas This Mister is the vengeance of disenfranchised men.

The muffled sound of bags being crumpled inward then rolled up; he tosses wads of plastic beneath with the accumulated detainees. He touches up all the defrosted pieces of poultry and puts them into an unoccupied compartment in the fridge.

Still life of assorted vegetables and lentils in a dish: the experimental nature of culinary arts is enjoyed on a completely different sensory. The taste of the human wit is carefully nurtured to serve excellence.

This Mister returns to the desk and fiddles with the zipper of the small compartment. Everything you can hope to make vanish on authoritative confrontation is contained within. Two bags of grass: a half-ounce of compact brick weed—stress bud obtained for javelin practice & the chronic: a half-eighth. There is also a foil wad he removes and pockets discretely; possession of LSD will get you attempted manslaughter *hence*...Suicide Inside (a working title).

He taps a Garcia-Vega green-leaf cigar from the bottom of the pencil slot stitched into the inside of the pocket. He tosses the cigarillo and the bulky sack on the table and puts the chronic in the fridge in the margarine compartment on his way back into the kitchen.

Returning to the table, he selects a chair in the back but not the furthest corner and takes a seat. He twists his dreads up momentarily while he struggles to overcome his preoccupation. A sense of worry registers in his eyes. The iris shrinks into obscurity. It is seemingly unapparent: the instigator of worry.

He awkwardly maneuvers out of the chair. It rolls back as he pushes himself out off it. He travels over to a three disc changer. It is beside a computer monitor besides the drafting table along the south wall. This Mister powers the device on.

He walks by the two minivan front passenger recliners situated on the floor around the tele. He crouches to read the titles of his audio media in a tower beside the dwarfish door.

He selects a disc from his Pink Floyd collection. He has the "Shine On" box set where the side of all the jewel cases completes the Dark Side emblem. He has also acquired every studio album "Obscured by Clouds" & "More". Their solo projects, a few live videos: he has two of three Roger Waters, a David Gilmour, and the infamous Madcap's laughter.

He pulls out "The Final Cut", opens up the CD shelf and sets the disc. He watches it spin in. He pushes stop as the CD closes up, making sure the aged & frequently uncooperative player reads the TOC. When he sees that it recognizes he pushes play. The first sounds of the album whisper by, traveling at a very high speed with direction. He throws his backpack behind a rocking chair at the end cap of the partition. It could have gone in the window of the racing car if its top had been dropped.

If everything ever said on those stairs could have been recorded— not as a joke but as heavy insight concerned with the liberation of human stature not to be dismissed. The next step would be to find a receptive audience. The grounds were timid and the air abroad intimidating. It's a foul way to describe it but you treason every promise alluding to grace.

* * 3 * *

In good grace—something he knows nothing of.

At least fitted into a comfortable position, he reaches for his for lone shaft sealed in plastic with a tab to unwrap it. The front left wheel of the chair rotates forward over the vertical axis, kicks around then, horizontally maneuvers the chair back to the drawers below the countertops. He opens the top drawer and fiddles through the strewn silver to retrieve an unshielded razor blade. He tenderizes the cigarillo with his salacious tongue. Absently he squeezes & examines it. He finds he can simply break it. There is no need for the razor blade. His break is relatively straight. He just pops it like a seam. The distasteful tobacco is shoved out over the trash can to his left.

First he's got to destem and deseed his weed because he doesn't have the funds—rather he doesn't feel exorbitant enough to spend the money on enough dank for chronic blunts. A honey bear is bonded to a coaster on the toaster near the sink until he gathers it. He holds the v-shaped tobacco leaf between his thumb and first finger then sprinkles the tiny spades and granular particles evenly across. One rollover then a little bit of honey as a tasty seal. It takes usually more than one tuck, and it is always easier to work from one end, keeping only the tips of the fingers in contact with the honey, as to prevent the attraction of little buds on the prints of the finger.

He places the blunt on an ashtray suspended by camels at three equidistant measurements of sixty degrees plotting an equilateral triangle. They have backward curved claws for humps. The concave tray is fastened to the camels atop their backs and beneath the claws.

The air will calm the wet paper in due time. He rolls his sack up, returns the honey, the razor blade, and discards all waste.

Only instantaneously can he enjoy his living spaces. Everything man does from the moment his obligations are met is his art. He can then begin on how to strategize his attack for an evening, or for the rest of his existence. The plan for this evening is to sulk in his selfish creativity & fantasies. He dies to live through them. Some of the sequences he exposes in his work.

The blunt won't be dry for a good five-7 minutes. Youth culture today depresses him. His experience, his high is vastly different from his contemporaries. He wishes he could've been a baby boomer. Instead he's a Reagan Baby. He was born in the Eighties.

The high for the person not searching to simply be stoned—on the verge of comatose, is worldly absolutely. So is taking the body of Christ.

LSD is ritualistic: a self-administered, self-delving psychoanalytic episode/journey/undertaking. LSD is capable of doing a great many things to a person. That possibly is the greatest understatement. This Mister is posing like questions. Wondering what it's all about. Why "The Final Cut" is so strung out.

He rises from his chair again to apprehensively take care of some business. He reaches into his pocket and retrieves the wad of foil kept on the D.L. He unfolds it. His hound dogs desire these delicious strips. He lays the strips of Einstein & Sunshine acid atop the counter. LSD is growing scarce in the central valley. However This Mister's manage to cop a variety. It took a while, some work, and tolerance of several lagging middle men to acquaint with a dealer. The shit should be lethal...not literally. The slits stare back like wild Zen Buddhists. He travels over to the ice box and retrieves the tropical punch concentrate; enhanced with one hundred-ten percent the daily recommended value of vitamin C.

He also retrieves a green half-size pitcher with a white spinning top that regulates pouring flow from: grated, to viscous, to restricted, by spinning its top. Next he retrieves out the chilled glass jug of water from the refrigerator. He raises it to wet his parched lips and wash out his cotton mouth & Saharan throat. Operating over the counter, he rips the cord of the concentrate container and pries the lid off. A fluid stream arcs out for an eyeballed measure as the deep maroon is diluted.

This pint sized pitcher is perfect for these fruit syrup medleys. He gives his head leeway to tilt back and raises the jug to the lips once more before returning the jug into a cooler ecosystem, the bio-carton if you will. He comes back around to the wing crest and this early bird swoops down for the *earthworm* in the open and scoops the strips with his tongue. He chews around in his mouth until it is soft enough to compress and settle under the tongue: an ice pack for that beautiful blue vein. Feel free to salivate as ye reek havoc on the frontal lobe.

He opens up a drawer and feels for the shape and texture until he has the desired wooden spoon in his grasp. Equipped, he stirs the liquid into a controlled whirlpool. Tear shaped driblets stretch as they plummet from the brink. He lets go of the spoon, hoping to see it be carried around in a whirlpool. Instead it is caught in the spout and is set to be swayed up and down with the current until the juice looses its momentum and can no longer force another revolution. During its diminishing cycles he pulls the spoon out and taps it on the rim. Bubbles whirl on the surface. He wipes his spoon with

Arnie's cushion towel and dabs up the miniscule overflow. He feels guilty setting the towel for Arnie's comfort because this is the last of Arnie the grapefruit tonight. It's a superficial world. It's Arnie's own fault for being aloof, perverse, & with his back against the wall.

The wooden spoon is set in the center atop the stove. He pours a glass of juice into the very concentrate can the frozen syrup was packaged in to save washing one dish. And then he puts the juice, after wrenching the handle to restrict flow out the spout, in the refrigerator and all the trash has already been disposed of at first regard. He still has not removed his shoes: it's about time.

He treads over to the table, peeking at the blunt, he walks over to the counter by the sink, wipes it down, there is nothing crumby on it. He repositions the honey coaster. There was nothing wrong with it. This Mister is neat but not usually a freak about it. He can't help being clumsy and less than coordinated to save his life. He's never actually been in a fight. All his battles unfold in his mind.

He turns over to the other corner, pressing time; it's wrinkle free. He ought to stop fussing. He's behaving like the widower in his dying days who still bothers to knot his socks.

Now he decides to sit.

He pulls the camel's carry towards him and examines the cigarillo.

He slides in the chair, stepping out from in front of a painted door he is blocking. He reaches into his pocket and pulls out a black Bic lighter. He softens his lips one more time He lavishes the cigarillo with another coat of saliva at the seam with pornographic sensuality and its trademark poor picture quality.

He sparks a flame at the end of the blunt tilted in a near eclipse of the eye, holding the flame steady. He releases the gas valve. With the ignited end near his slightly parted lips, winds whisper to stoke the embers of the lamppost with a lava top. He mouths the end piece, smacks his lips and puffs a golden spiral cloud out before his face. This Mister tokes the post, then removes it and holds it before him, not frozen or yet stoned, but still; like contemplative manners are fashionable. He settles the post into a slot between his middle and ring finger in his left hand; elbow propped on the table. Then he leans back in his seat. Sights down the blunt, over the lava top and watches the whispers of smoke rise before his face and just above his head where the wisps coil like coral in the still air. He returns the shaft to the pouting perch to stick to the skin where the meat of the lower lip is.

Every rip flickers up the intensity of the cherry. Small bubbles of smoke evade from the corners of his chops. He detaches the post from his perch and stares at the cherry reflecting white off his eye.

We think we are dissecting the truth when we pose on the steps and talk in chains of progressing thought. We refine all the things we know. We take notes from visual process and etch what we read and what we hear so that we can incorporate it into our repertoire. The wrinkles in our brain catalogue impressions to be accessed imaginatively in the future when seeking to create or in need of inspiration. The vision of enlightenment is bringing the unbridled subconscious beast into the civilized pastures of conscious and to begin conditioning. This is reasonably pursuing authenticity.

* * 4 * *

This Mister blows smoke from the lungs in a corner chair. Behind him is a solid door he won for six dollars in an auction painted by a local underground artist. This solid door was wrestled from dumpsters behind a random apartment complex as all of that Artist's panels are acquired.

A blue green torpedo hangs in the closet, looming over a bald sea green man's head. It is suspended in dismay. There is no body allotted to this meat head, pasted on an uneven multi-toned red backdrop. Dismayed Dad's eyes have been sewn shut. The features of his head are strongly demarcated. Blood trickles from his lower lip and drips off his chin.

Besides the hung up torpedo a banner is dropped. It is fixed up with the markings of a befuddled bystander who rests both elbows and his left forearm atop a table. A martini glass, complete with pimento olive & tooth pick speared through is in arms reach. His right forearm is lifted back against his bicep. This idiot savant apathetically points at the hung up torpedo like, *"what's with the snow cone maker?"*

A figure which looks like a no-stringed banjo with arms and a head hovers over the floor space. It appears to be holding a séance over a fire which could be roasting Dismayed Dad's head like a green marshmallow. With its toothpick arms and slender, oversized fingers pointing, the Hovering Figure orders its heart out of the sound hole and into the flames.

Eatchoveggies takes it there. Throw your heart out. This Mister's trash can is right against the door, covering the fire in the lower right corner. It looks the heart is being reassigned to the wastebasket. Which is worse? Is it wondrous: the irony?

There's more to the solid panel closet scene. There are two brief, few-frame comic exchanges. Maybe they will seem relevant later on. If not...regardless, This Mister & Eatcho are obviously at a loss.

However this loss imposes little to no effect upon This Mister. He knows the bomb won't drop on him. He's fifty percent Caucasian. He's accustomed to middle class privilege. He could be going to a university. His grades certainly render him worthy of scholarly opportunities. Instead he makes a living renting movies and collecting late fees...and he reads: Shakespeare, Dostoyevsky, Dante, etc. It's like...he's totally secure. His guts only wrench in these quarters because he forces on the cold & sore in pursuit of the comfortably numb. "No one kills the children anymore" belts Roger Waters out over the minimal audio accompaniment: great cold war memorabilia.

It is what it is: significance? There's only one inquisition. Figure for yourself.

Atop the drafting table is a wicker basket with various oil paints: vermilion red, ebony, antique white, burnt umber, burnt sienna, and a cadmium yellow hue. He notices the following hues: Sap green, French ultramarine, and yellow ochre, rummaging through before he handles the basket. He returns to the corner where he's enjoying quality minutes of mourning, huddling around the ashtray. He reclaims the lava lamppost.

A cardboard palette sticks outside the basket, hardly distinguishable. It is ripped from a discarded box in the shape of an ellipse with a ducktail. He rips off some paper towels and retrieves a clouded salsa jar of soaking brushes from the nub of a counter beside the sink. Bestowing the blunt back unto his lips, he maneuvers back to this area about the table and sorts through the brushes. Shortly he's selected three of varying girth & shape and pats them in paper towel cupped around the bristles. Navy blue blotches of dirty water heavily stain the generic quilted fiber towel.

He clears his way, guiding the chairs aside to group around the other side, to move into the very back corner. He strokes the wall up around and about. He uncaps the burnt umber tube squeezes the first glob of oil paint onto the wall, scraping the wall in a downward arcing motion.

This Mister's stimulated mind, intuitively creative, applies the brush to texture the arc with braids. He began this stroke from the corner and has taken it down to his waist. He scrapes an ebony line horizontally from the endpoint into the corner. Then he peers through the tunnel with his vision. He perceives a path through and bending around the corner with an upwards grade as if it were the spiraling slide one must drive up to the top of a parking garage: narrow and walled in, at least it will be once he's painted his vision.

He picks up the blunt to hold it for keeps in the crevice between his fingers, spread in a sign of peace. He uncaps the antique white and with a bigger and much more brittle brush bats the white onto his brush then mixes it on the wall with the ebony. Once he acquires a dolphin gray consistency he duplicates it on the cardstock palette. From here he applies to pave the illusion of a street winding around into the depths from nine onto twelve o'clock. He lays a second coat of jet black over the thinly outlined and shaded roadway He's covering with the ebony because he's decided instead to use the dolphin gray to denote the routed tunnel wall arching over.

Continuing to elevate his awareness, to induce the full potency of the fry, he recovers the burnt umber and scratches a few marks onto the wall. The marks fence the road in as the width of the pavement diminishes into the distance. Next he marks out a pillar in the foreground in the corner. Reequipping the burnt umber tube, he throws a stubby vertical line that shoots away from the pillar onto the adjacent wall. He continues carrying and curving just beyond the parameters of the pocketed sector before abruptly rolling down and then tucking in below the pocket like a tummy is sucked in below the rib cage: in this case the pocketed tunnel. It is suddenly apparent that he's outlined an oddly human head. It seems crudely to be smashed in by the corner of the wall. An indentation that presumably in this light must signify the bridge of the nose is directly above what must be the tip of the nose that initially seemed to be nothing more than the base of a cylindrical pillar. The nose appears broken. It's odd that the person's face should be so smashed into the wall, maybe the figure is on a time-out.

He squints at this image before him discerning while he tokes until his senses flare. There is adequate room under the braded arc between his pavement and the corner where a pillar has been converted into or doubles as a nose. He dares to dab some yellow ochre over his cardboard palette, switches back to the first brush and rolls it over the dung heap then commences painting declaratively.

Totally unaware of how impulsively he renders, he steps back from a release of spastic energy that left him the side view of the checks of a pathetically masculine face. The yellow ochre with the tonal deepness of sunflower or pollen mixes well with the umber and traces of gray. He notices particularly a squinting eye and thin lips. A detached portrait, alas it is scratched and there are grayish yellow welts around his temples. He appears tired of being.

Thinking about it while he puffs the phalange that he tokes down to a nub: he is confused by how everything forms irrelevantly. Life is unintended. Circumstance is the victim of consequence.

Is This Mister a victor?

Is This Mister a star? Neither. Probably.

How many truly are?

This Mister belongs to a demographic of young men without fathers to reel them in. The threat without originates within. He doesn't understand it.

Instead he turns around looking at the dome light in the middle of the kitchen ceiling. He should change it out and shut off these electric candles overhead perched on the chandelier. There should be a red shroud to soil his despair.

He grabs the carton with the red party bulb and maneuvers around the crowd of chairs, flips off the candle light by the switch in the partition behind where the honey bear is lined up amongst mostly souvenir bottles and bar glasses on the counter. He then sneaks around the counter and into the corridor until he's under a ceiling lamp. He reaches up to unscrew the tiny threaded holding screws so he can slide the glass bubble off. He must rotate around the bubble to do so; barely able to reach. He stretches his body and rises onto his toes. Smoke clouds his face. The acid has taken effect, enhancing his sense of balance. He unscrews the burnt out light bulb and lobs it towards the can, aiming to toss it just over the countertop's rightwing. It may have missed and broken on the ground. He's not sure, he could be hallucinating.

Fitting the bulb in along the threads until it buts against to complete the circuit, he stimulates the filament with electrons passing along the element strung between two ends of a wishbone like apparatus. Blood stained cells spread into the atmosphere and this hue will dominate space for possibly the remainder of the evening. It's a perfect accessory for paranoiac midsummer night single suicide party. He carefully places the glass sphere meant to protect under the sink, rather than have it dull the crimson hue staining every surface and object within. The glass bubble is now jail bait.

An ideal pot for heating soups in is stored in a single metallic drawer beneath the oven. The long appendage of a handle is broken off so the pot when it is hot must be clasped around the rim through a towel. He coughs as he bends down to open the drawer that crashes with its metal guidelines as it slides out noisily. It pierces like a gash by his lobes, bolting against his ear drums. The first peak of a rock 'n' roll saga has struck its chord. He feels definitely the presence of an instigator.

The blunt is about the stature and size of a medium-large cockroach so he lays the finished dream maker back to rest in the Arabian ashtray. There's a can-opener in the first drawer where the silver splash. He searches to retrieve it presently.

The gears of this contraption saw around the lid the garbanzo tin because he's cranked the handle and now into the stout cylinder front left he pours the legumes sizzling as they strike the solid scorching floor of the pot absorbing the energy expended from the turquoise flames. He pours half of the can into the pan. The beans have filled the pan like marbles in a dish, every single one beside the other. He retrieves a lemon from the stockpile, sweet Citrus, is introduced to a maliciously delinquent blade summoned form the third drawer of army recruits: they; they've all been in the shit, used to slice shit up like a rainbow roll. They are privates with distant gazes and hysterical retinas. Well, they have this quality attributed to them since obviously they are inanimate kitchen utensils. They are guerillas however, don't be deceived. This maggot paring knife is pressured into slicing through the large and firm lemon held over the sink, but not directly over the bowl of lentils.

This Mister whisper's as he slits her, "sweet Citrus, you're not an ambassador, it's just a name."

He pulls out a glass measuring cup from the cupboards above then turns around with two lemon halves in his right hand to retrieve a plastic yellow juicer from the drawer just above the legion of shanks.

He fits this over the measuring cup to catch the juice running down the vertically cut canyons between the ridges circumscribing the juicer. The liquid citrus squeeze and stringy citrus flesh clings to the slits in the bottom of the moat circumscribing the ribbed horn, erect to juice the vestal flesh. At last the liquid's tensile strength relinquishes to weight and the liquid plummets & splatters.

By & by Citrus tears drizzle through, by, or with the ravaged flesh of the fruit and makes soft sounding placid impacts on the bottom. He snags a garlic flower, partially plucked on some or several occasions previous. It's on the counter right before him. He's never bought garlic. He always pockets it while he's at the store. His father tried to put the fear of law into him when he was younger. It didn't work. He enjoys the thrill of stealing necessities. Perhaps for some garlic is a frivolity but he's Lebanese, onion, lemon, and garlic color everything. His father would always talk about how grateful he was to have ONE cookie before bed time and he used to declare that in Lebanon they made their own toys. He was pious with a passion. He would never resort to thievery. Once in his youth This Mister was caught with stolen merchandise when it came out of his pocket at home while he was on the sofa and his mother was asking him something of no consequence. His father instantly attracted the fury of nations and threatened to contact the police and the store management until This Adolescent was on his knees pleading and screaming and bawling. The fear didn't last. Dismayed Dad was too embarrassed to shuttle some Life Savers back. A couple years later he would pass. A couple years later This Mister would grab & dash Skyy vodka, CDs, peaches, and the like.

He pries two buds from the garlic flower then allows it to slip out of his hands and land with a thud back on the counter. So what though? The flower is solid matter, not paper mâché, like the petals of a flowering species. Besides, the garlic clove doesn't bruise, like this overtly sensitive inexperienced man:

a depressing flower with a poem about how—possibly he will share with you that which he is in ways. He smashes each clove under the blade of the paring knife, then rips both the knotted ends of each clove off with his thumb nail, and finally peels off the flaky skin off. He turns quickly to retrieve the mortar and pestle from the same cupboard as the measuring cup, and also grabs the salt container from the pantry. He pours a pinch of salt over the peeled cloves in the mortar and begins to pummel with the pestle.

Immediately the garlic begins to excrete an odorous mist as its hull is stomped and this bud is thrashed. He leaves the pestle standing perpendicular then grabs the measuring cup. He pours the lemon juice into the mortar then picks up the pestle, newly doused, and scrapes off the clinging garlic with his manic blade.

The red light: frightfully dim, leaves the wood orange, and makes the walls glow. Every feeling is pubescent. Every urge is primal. Fear & loathing is the discipline. It's simple, really. This Mister's only wish is to cop-out because only through becoming your father do you grow up. He doesn't want to take over the business. He moved out because he hasn't the tenacity to move to SF: the bay area. He's only been on his own in paradise four months. Mom, look at him now.

Presently he pours the tangy dressing in the mortar over the pot of boiling garbanzo beans. After pivoting and a few paces later he stoops before his pantry to pick up a three liter jug of oil.

He grabs his trusty wooden spoon, lying around from when he last used it to stir the punch he's yet to splash his throat with. This spoon is the most versatile, most preferred kitchen utensil for all manner of jobs and taste-tests. He feels nearly joyous just to use it in the passing of time engaged in this most satisfying activity.

All the fuss is settled once he applies his stirring care. He ushers the chick peas all over and around the cylinder. He spoons two beans to taste test and dials the burner off. Then grabs a piece of pita from the fridge, cracks the oven, set it to broil, and tosses the coin of bread through the slot like a piece of mail or a Frisbee. It's the same motion. This Mister attends for an indeterminable span of time, with his eyes closed, stroking the hair on his chin, tapping his foot to the "The Final Cut".

It must have been a minute, possibly two. His envoy is not burnt when he retrieves it. It's hot though. He potatoes it back and forth, then finally flings it onto the table. It lands at the front edge and slides near to his drink container. He acquires a synthetic wood bowl then pats Arnie to assure the lonesome grapefruit before he borrows his blankie. He grips the pot with the towel as a glove and scoops a portion into his bowl. Then he returns Arnie's blankie for him to be kept on. Blankie's are for cowards who want but can't handle. This Mister then drifts back to the table: a boy who thinks he is hungry, a boy who thinks he can eat.

He settles down in his seat and stares absently at his dish; particularly the bean spread. After a few stretched moments he reaches without looking out and behind him and fingers for the top drawer. He wraps his fingers around, slides it open and identifies a spoon, as blind as his eyes are closed. Once the spoon is in his grasp and held above the bowl, he hesitates no more. He scoops his spoon and holds the first full load near his upper lip to gauge its temperature. He smiles in gaiety, slurps the tangy appetizer, & chews.

He rips the bread in half across, tears a wedge the size and relative shape of a blunt garden spade then tears the bread at the pocket seam. Now he has two pieces. He then folds one piece in half, holding flaps open and horizontal like a tray. He next makes a partial fold from the back straight over. Needless to say he's put down his spoon because now he has a bread scoop. He now can sail vessel after vessel into the cavity of his mouth. Garlic mist stream of breath is nothing because there's no one around to kiss. His breath smells fine; he wafts off the palm of his hand—like strawberries or sweets. He goes off to thinking the last time he kissed was the last time he cried. He holds his head in his left thumb & forefinger.

Intention is blind and therefore we believe it comes from nowhere. Therefore out of nowhere This Mister reaches for the punch and socks it down his throat, for more than one swallow. When he is done and has brought the container back down onto the table he keeps a hold of it in his left hand. His forearm lain across the table attached to his wrist looks mildly like an immobilized specimen. How hard must he try to forget it's attached?

He continues to eat releasing his grip on the cup and firmly wrapping his fingers around the spoon, he continues to plunge, but stop. He wants to stop eating. Maybe it's just the spoon. Maybe he wants to spoon Kate Chopin—maybe that's not such a stretch. He is awakening.

He was in a trance, never mind.

He rips another wedge of bread which is still more than half of the original round. He folds through and dips it in his bowl then lifts the vessel. The light that shines in his crimson cup spins around and touches the acute arcs of light nestled across from each other against the borders like a ping-pong game but this one has been turned down to light sound.

"The Final Cut" has thoroughly flayed. The Water of words sings in a stream "foe and friend/they were all equal in the end". You have no idea who he misses and what he dreads. This Mister couldn't tell you what he wants. He wants to watch "Good Will Hunting" again. You don't even know what 'The Final Cut' sounds like and This Mister didn't bother to relate it to you, or what he was doing hardly. He hardly, he can only suggest, pick it up if you want to feel as old and strung out as Cold War survivors. He didn't even sing along. Right now his chin is resting on the butt of his hand. His elbow is on the table. The vessel is set down into the bowl. The bread is soggy.

He carries the bowl to the sink intent on washing it out. The sense of bad manners strikes him. He rubs his brows, doesn't know what to say, & even though he's not doing anyone any favors he finishes his meal...Quickly, within the time it took to type those three dots. The unused portion in the can is preserved in the refrigerator. He can't wash his dishes out without doing something with the soaking lentils. The drawer rollers of the metal drawer beneath the oven screech and scrape along. It occurs to him this space probably heats up when the oven is on. Surely heat is transferred along and/or through metals.

Touché

This Mister is his own formidable opponent who gains knowledge by the day and night. It probably is a warming locker or a bread warmer or for pies. Or for storage—oh well. Just...you wouldn't open a door if the knob was hot.

He sets a stew pot on the back right burner and pours the lentils in so he can rinse out his dishes. All apologizes. This Mister doesn't mean to bore you with the menial.

Oh did he break the fourth wall—well while he's drawn his own door with a Faun's chalk might as well drop knowledge—it comes in either ink or bombs.

Da Vinci wrote in his notebook with his left hand—and that's not all. Da Vinci wrote in his notebook "To conceive an idea is noble. To execute the work is servile" with his left hand.

See the relevance? Come on don't be a pacifist. Of course we're in league. You've been lured now...don't stray. Not everything foul produces regret.

The pot is already holding water, as the lentils were soaking in a metal dish in an inlet over the sink. Nevertheless he fills the glass measuring cup with water. There still is a lemon coat for sure on the glass but it is so diluted obviously, and it wouldn't ruin anything. It's not worth noticing but he's aware. He pours a talon of water long enough for the lentils to be submerged approximately 5/8 in. The burner is dialed to medium heat, the pilot clicks, and then a spark ignites. Surface units are hot albeit low. Now he can clean out the bowl before his audience goes into a fit over it—wait. It's too early for the lentils to be on. It'll be almost an hour before he really starts cooking. So he turns the pilot off.

Now that everything is clean and he knows what he'll need he freely peers around; scanning the room. The surfaces appear awesomely different than those plain off-white plastered panels two-three hours ago. Grades of red glow atop each surface uniquely. His eyes run up the rings on the wood surfaces; red as bold as crimson—keeping beat. Keeping heart beat.

He cannot depict for you the tessellated arrangements growing bolder the longer his shut eyes are held firmly. He cannot choreograph for you the movement of the forces in space. He cannot depict decently what it looks like to see gusts of shuttling vapors or the way air gathers around a tree, a chair, or anything. He cannot paint for you his aura on the page with words. He could try and descriptively analyze and create however it would likely be horribly cumbersome, uninteresting, and long. Which is why he will merely relate his impressions if he can utter them as profound as they occur mentally before they are fit definitively with symbols. He cannot clue you into to any mysteries of the universe. He may have led you on but only because he's starved for attention; a forgivable offence, no?

There are letters in the visuals. He does recognize them in the print hovering above the surface. He has yet to make out any word which...boggles his mind.

Does this qualify as a mystic experience?

* * 5 * *

The pixilated peach colored surface of the porcelain sink captured This Mister's attention. What is nectar? What is citrus? As a symbol people can get behind.

He doesn't blink.

Atop the tissue toned glow over the porcelain, purple and green bolts and zagging lines dart and/or trot across the walls and lap around the basin. They remain shorter than the shortest straw: on second thought maybe they're inflated bacterium. They can be whatever he wants to see. Little pastel quality fags; actually bundles of nail clippings are hyperactive in this bed; shooting everywhere. Some creatures just flash and remain basically stationary but most of these bent tails squirm or beam about to places.

He really is interested. He should have checked the odd, but something in him helps him to break from the sink and back step to the counter; head over his right shoulder. A jet black cutting board, slightly larger than the standard sheet of paper is leaning against the refrigerator behind Arnie. Arnie makes a good monument.

Flakes are scattered all over it. Although they are not arranged in constellations as he examines the board he notices the random pinholes splattered do sparkle like gems. They appear to bob above the surface of the plane and then slip into the board—that is when he slides the board, his little black monolith with constellations atop the counter. He is about to get ill on this onion.

He chooses a lengthy blade plenty sleek: the corporal of knife ware. With force he cuts the knotted ends of the onions and stands them at the right side of the board naked—that is, with the driest and some flimsy outer layers peeled away.

Here this amateur begins; he bisects through the plateaus leveled. To keep from the power of the stench crying his eyes, he breathes through his mouth. He begins to dice. All the widths of fan-shaped onion slices are even, 1/8 inch. Don't be surprised. He may be frying, but he can cook. To do something naturally is better than to do something well.

With a swiftness he's switched back already and requisitioned a yellow Tupperware bowl. He flips it over and settles it down onto the counter behind the board where there's barely enough room left. To tell the truth all the fruit is getting a little squished.

He calculates a moment to dispel wonder. He asked himself: wonder how much food will be left minus the share you prepare. This Mister reckons he ought to prepare for at least three. Hopefully no one from the ministry will show their suspecting face unannounced, black bag & pounce. Paranoia: the effects of media?

An intriguing thesis—care to elaborate?

He's sliced through these onions now. They are a bunch of arching segments concentrically arranged and sticking together by natural mucus mortar. He scoops the wedges resembling paper fans. With the greatest ease he breaks them up with busy fingers as they shower down, out of his grasp into the bowl before him.

It's early still; he needs the onions to chill in the fridge. so when he's in front facing it he yanks the handle and moves out of the way for the door to swivel beside him. Artificial light is astonishingly bright. One fluorescent light monetarily blinds then dissipates into the engulfing & prevailing shade of the district, more appropriately quarters.

Don't mind This Mister. All authors solicit connotation.

This Mister picks up the fruit juice container and swallows a hearty amount to follow up, because he's still uncertain about how to transition best into what to be preoccupied with next.

* * 6 * *

He steps out of the grim glow of the kitchen into the twilight shrouding the den. Perhaps some music but what sort of brain tease?

"Won't you be my Atom Heart Mother?" he speaks with a little bit of a trot, like a warm up. He however restrains himself short of breaking into a dance with his front passenger minivan bucket seats. It's so hard to dance when you are cold and it's better to zone to some types of music. He preps the remastered Floyd relic to play in the compact media driver. For some reason the driver has a difficult time reading the Table of Contents. Positively he has a backup plan. Through the computer he can play compact discs.

He wakes the computer from its hibernating state; aggravating the mouse. He opens the bottom disk drive and inserts his disk, then puts enough force against the tray for it to retract. The CD initiates automatically he switches his media unit to auxiliary so he still hears the program out of the speaker cabinets towering above against the banister.

While the sound slowly begins to warm the space with the call of trumpets and the distant roar of dragsters the young man walking away approaches his project and selects one of the chosen brushes, dabbing it with the towel while preparing mentally what is timely but perhaps not vogue.

He dusts the west wall with his fingerprints. He expresses his deepest regrets for the condition of the creature's nose on the adjacent wall. It is somewhat permanent. It began as a clandestine operation to delve into the information highway of a mind. It's the person's fault for being the type of accessory that would allow it to become collateral damage.

How's that paranoia thesis progressing?

He paints a solid line over the area he's waxed his fingerprints over with a brush about as big and full as the middle segment of his pinky. He continues to sketch a rectangular box, longer than it is tall. This box is composed of wavering lines that look like a hung sheet or a cross section of a collapsed carton. In This Mister's defense he's not using a yarn covered mallet to steady his hand. He's nobody's apprentice. It appears that wind blows or again a crushed prism is in suspense. Because he understands geometry, understands perspective, he can make attempts at constructing the illusory nature of dimension. This is not a bar a soap, this is not a slate of wood; this is not a sheet of bronze. This is a wall. Fuck the property managers. He's painting on the wall.

He rounds out the bottom right corner and details it as if brushing in a goatee. A goatee fashioned into three claws becoming sharper. It appears now as a whole: a rock formation filled out. Now he gives the rough chin a profile. It is a slender ovular face, apparently turning to face. He finishes it off with a cross hatched nose.

Afterwards he trades for a fine tip brush shaped like a hair lick. He uncaps the yellow ochre, allocates a small heap to his palette, and dabs into the solid oil log then paints two coin slots eye level approximately. The difference in size from right to left is such that one could accept a quarter, the other merely a dime. Next This Mister dabs the brush into a little bit of the crud colored black he has left, drying on the cardboard palette and devastates the portrait. He paints from the tear duct along and across the nose, a scarring sliver which traverses the cheek and follows along just as if it were an outgrown mustache though it doesn't have that amusing upward curve. It is wretched. It is hideous. This cannot be a face of an American. This portrait must be of some raped Bosnian. It's that crude. It has none of the elegance of a real woman. The cross hatch—it must be cat claws.

Apparently undisturbed he continues by weaving a wig. The hair is matted and dirty blond. There is black, ash, soot. This Mister wipes the brush and shapes the whites of the eyes. There are no questions asked, he does not appear terrified. Not a bead of sweat appears on his brow. Suddenly perturbation sweeps over his face in a wave. Are her eyes lactating? He scribbles in some wrinkles and does injustice to her cheeks revealing the features of a flat faced young lady with sunken cheeks, bad color, and bad skin. Some washed apricot would make her look exceptionally pale. First she needs lips tight & drawn in as if by an internal suction drive.

"I bet you used to know a whole fucking lot!"

This Mister has to bite his own lip not to spit upon her. He pivots his head and bats his eyes as if to scold himself. This is only the result of ugly treatment. She is a victim. This Mister has harnessed predatorily instincts. It is his prerogative whether to repress or embellish—not to imply these are only two avenues towards an end point. This Mister needn't even be resolute.

He wipes his slender brush again, than squeezes some vermillion red to his palette beside his smear of varying shades of gray. He's going to give this young battered woman old gray lips like she's been rationed cement passed off as grits. Now the emotional benevolence of the character is revealed. Her lips are slender but they're not pursed. He tsks. He truly feels confused about what he's trying to achieve. He is confused; on the verge of repulsion. One little hint of humanity. She has no fear. She is free. That is the conclusion he draws.

This Mister moves on. He moves over on the panel, the horizontal totem. There's no sleep to lose, it's not like he'll have to battle these images in the afterlife...as far as This

Mister knows everything in this life gets bent. That's the price of balance.

They're perfect together...as bookends: the wretched pair. He's not going to paint anything in between.

* * 7 * *

This is what it has come to: doubt; suddenly if it seems that way. The innovative ambition to delve into the mystery of the psyche has been pooped out. It's time to forget, time to abate, and time to relinquish if This Mister says so.

He washes his hands off in the empty inlet, taking the time as well to bring some water to his face. Vegetables in the sink have been thoroughly dampened. He bobs for the parsley pulls the bunch out and squeezes the leaves sensually like he once squeezed a sponge to get just the right amount of liquid from the tub flow down his lover's back. Then he finger banged her as she faced him with her wisteria eye shadow and her quivering lips and her shrill whine. He was timid at first to undress her even though they openly confessed their desire to bathe with, to the other. It was beautiful then, it is unbearable now? Where is the comfort? Don't others give unconditionally?

"We were the last two matches in a book Love—what's the story?" He speaks with increasing fervor until the last inquisitive remark is exclaimed. This Mister is not unnerved by the silence, he's accustomed.

This Mister has lessons to learn, however there is to be no more experiences to bless him with this understanding he's declared because he feels life to be so cumbersome lately waking in the morning sick from weak or terrible dreams.

Venus: the Roman goddess of love proves to be a cold, barren carcass on the regular. It's sickening. One strand flutters back into the pond, he pays it no mind, although he can't say he doesn't notice it. He doesn't make a scene around it; he is too bloated to regard it—moving on. Here he is run ashore. Can he viably say he was marooned? This Mister wants to.

He curses this fix under his breath. He fetches two sheets of paper towel; enough to settle gently the flakes of parsley onto a quilted pad atop untempered coil. The oven door is still on and propped open. Through the crack are seeping poisonous gases. This Mister is content to work over and waft in. But he'd like to live through his dinner. He's expecting company. So he shuts the oven off and closes the hatch, then looks carefully around to mind the shadows in the foreground.

Just inside the threshold of the pantry on the ground is a Cuisineart food processor. All the fruit is brushed back so the machine can halfway fit on the counter. He plugs the device into the wall socket just behind. He removes the lid with an elliptical chimney. He begins to pick the leaves from each individual branch of each strand. He flicks and brushes the wet leaves the size and shape of green pencil shavings from his fingers to flutter sadly and slowly down into the dish. When he is half way through the parsley he shifts his attention to the mint leaves that are still in the sink. He attains the bunch and shakes them once over the sink. He rips a handful of leaves from their stems savagely like he's tearing away a chunk of ground beef to make a patty and drops the bunch atop the parsley on the towel. He then tears and rips and rolls, shreds and molests the leaves in his devouring hands before he discards them in long tatters above the accumulating parsley shavings in the dish. Next he picks out the stems and grooms them intently placid for a few moments before thrashing only the inedible. It's just a few steps back from, before Mehran's painted door skin in which he fiddles through a schism: a premonition a warning, in his mind tells him to desist. He will not desist. He's only on six hits of acid. What's the worst that could happen? He fits the lid on; snaps it into place: snap.

Pulse: he's depressed the lever and holds. The contents are shot to the wall spinning around the carousel consistently they fall out of cyclical movement and are emulsified. The noise from revolving blade sends his head spinning and prompts a palpitation of the heart. He lets up on it compulsively. A few seconds go by frame by frame, sixteen per second. In the last moments he operates in bursts so the contents are not minced to liquid negligently. It's funny that This Mister has the sensibility to do this because he feels really lightheaded. He discontinues the pressure and the spin slows, the noise subsides, and his spinning head has a chance live out momentum. The conscious settles in a hazy environment of purple and lime bursts.

To understand self, to understand the work, and the inner workings so to reason through impulses is essential to the human being, and especially the artist. Go to sit upon the stairs and examine all the angles. Tonight the alchemist is lone, though this was not necessarily so in past excursions. But the time for collective input seldom sees through anymore.

He finds himself gripping the front of the counter of the sink hunched over and wheezing for oxygen to breathe. What is this? Why is he here? He gathers his sense of position, catches his breath.

He needs to get a big bowl to put the first portions of the salad in. He opens up the dishwasher placed in the counter aside the sink. No there is nothing in there. What is he thinking? All the bowls are over the stove. He opens the cupboard and reaches for the white salad bowl. While pulling down the selected dish he bumps the handle of a yellow plastic strainer bowl and sends it tumbling down into his pile of greens. His grasp never weakened. He didn't flinch, but he's irritated on account he's confused.

"What is this becoming a circus?" He looks to the carousel and buttons his lip then shrugs. This Mister is having fun. He replaces the fallen strainer, closes the cabinet overhead and proceeds to unfasten the lid: click.

He pulls off the blade carefully from its counterpart. He unsnaps the dish, grabbing by its handle. He empties the contents into the bowl using the wooden spoon. Then he begins anew, reassembling the contraption and loading it for round two with a certain calm composure, he didn't have a moment ago. The leaves flutter there way into the can like butterflies that have no reason for concern. He takes the time to notice and develop a simile in regards.

The stems are given their jolly discord in the trashcan. The doomsday machine has been replenished. It is to be reactivated under strong discord. The closing lid is securely snapped to fasten: pulse.

The fallout is worse. He intently depresses. The red light is a deviant instigator; suggesting the contrary. The fear that prompts him is masculine; it is driven by testosterone. He knows beads of sweat want to drench him. He is only beginning to glisten. Apprehension is rising, his eyes are bugging. Time is jumbled to such a degree it's passage makes eternity look like a class period. It seems as if an instant occupies an era. He is directly inside this epoch: bursting in the end—faster! Shred that parsley! Be all the dervish you can be—and...release!

He holds his ground, cranial pressure is causing anxiety. He slips up in the kitchen—heated, and releases—flails, unable to recover. He falls out of his role as rider, collapses into the cabinet beneath the sink abruptly. Something shatters, it sounds like glass within the cabinet possibly. This Mister is naught but a drilled little unconscious boy on the linoleum who's banged his head. The machine must have stopped itself. He makes a mental note; sending regards. Either there's a God or an automatic stop on the device. He stands to the decision that he won't pulse on the whirlwind another time. Then he realizes he's finished anyways. He unclasps the lid. What an experience: it was a pure uncanny whip. It gives him pause. He tries to sense some mental growth to indicate some degree of attained light in the aftermath. He hastily unlatches the dish after fetching up the blade. He scrapes the dish dry with his hand like a paw, rather than civilly with his favored wood spoon. He gathers it around into mounds, actually the butt off his hand is flexible, perhaps more efficient. It's his crazed demeanor that bungles his effectiveness.

Finally he looks at the parsley that looks like a deep green chewed moss in the white bowl with a marine blue bottom. Then suddenly he is reminded, and shudders into haphazardly venturing to rinse the debris from the lid and removable dish, as well as the blade then, frantically wiping them with the cloth towel he whisks from under Arnie who rolls off the counter this time and is stepped on reactively with a firm stomping heel. Arnie's flesh surely scatters. This Mister has just committed an act of malice. He returns the Cuisineart stepping on or over him.

He lets out a sigh of relief but nervously thrusts his hands in under the running water. He lifts water in his cupped palms to his faces and splashes it then massaging along the ridge of his nose washes down. He wails "y'Allah forgive me Allah". It's something he'd hear his father shout in moments of despair with all the passion of the Fertile Crescent. He knows, he is well aware that only through becoming your father do you grow up. In some but not all cases it entails taking up the profession chivalrously. But the business—ah the business is the antithesis of the brier patch. Or it is the brier patch and This Mister is not the Brier Rabbit; or the best of both nightmares.

* * 8 * *

He reaches into the cabinets above the stove and the vent for his bong. The water is clean enough; he holds the glass like it contains fine bubbly. It will bubble suitably: inspire him to play on words notably. He pulls out his chronic buds from the butter compartment in the refrigerator. He has to rid the grinding sensation from his head. His gears need lubrication.

He dumps the sack out of the bag onto a tray on the counter under the light switch. On the tray is a Lebanese castle with a vaguely familiar but unrelated family posing before a monumental castle. He pinches up some of the herb and packs a bowl. Then This Mister maneuvers to the table and sits down to look at the painting or at least, to be near enough to think about it with his back actually turned to the newly soiled west wall. He's right in front of Mehran's work again in the same seat.

Atom Heart Mother is five tracks long and the first is an overture twenty four minutes long—and its over. The second is entitled 'if'. 'If' deals mostly with the archetype of a good man. It cues up at a perfect time. He grabs his lighter and puts the bong to his mouth. The smoke fills up in dense spiraling cloud pockets filling the spout. He pulls the bowl from the down-stem and clears the bubble chamber his palm wraps around below the smoke rising in the spout towards his ridiculously cupped mouth.

He holds the hit in, Blood rushes by his temples, the lobes intrigued. He fights against the urge to bellow, sipping in little bits of air until desperately he surrenders and in several harsh coughs, his lungs baritone the smoke: expelling. His head is thrown back but not against the door. His coughs become progressively shorter and less raspy. He raises the back of his left hand to his brow, while the right clenches the spout of the bong on his knee. His inner conscious comes to vein.

Mystical epiphanies conjured while tripping on the case reveals order ambiguously. Any habitual process that shapes you is a form of spiritual reckoning. No one was born to live for their death. Live through life, experience life, in all perspectives to find contentment. Careful the abominating power of regret; courageously pursue intrigue. Don't live in fear of people, scorning things, neglecting books you should read, shrugging off places you'd die to see. Don't try to die. Don't wish to leave life. Be true. Be smart, or be taken by predicaments and visions you never prepared for. Like the visage of foot hills, over which a dark gray winged beast with a blue violet hue swoops through nimbus clouds and pollutants in the sky. Approaching…descending.

Flooding crimson saturates elongated yet slender storm clouds and stains the ether between as the plasma bleeds. Plasma bleeds, therefore it's fiery. A dark star revolves; climbing over like Apollo brings his chariot to the zenith from the horizon. The grim twilight is horrific.

There's nothing going on outside. He jumps out of his hallucination. Roger Waters laments of the spaces between friends and if only to be a moon to be cruel.

What time is it?

It's twilight. This Mister is pretty fried out like the most commercial fried eggs. He's peaking so early in the evening. This is the night.

He stands and picks up the round mounded brush all soiled in umber and ochre. He reckons it's time to paper dry them so he rips off a sheet, actually he's already got one on the table from some time ago but it is too late he's already done the deed and as wiping not all the oil off but some. The bristles are with just a rustic stain upon them now. He doesn't have any turpentine to use. He's not trying to impress anybody. He looks around at his first composition. It looks like there's a forward arcing alfalfa or a fishing pole emanating from the cow lick. It's from the original arc he scraped. The tunnel didn't occupy the whole space. Therefore there was room for the face in the corner. It looks incomplete. But This Mister sees the future of such a rendering therefore it is already complete.

He lobbies for some new paint. He needs to post some phrase up. He needs a worthy hue. Red-orange he can do with some vermillion red and cadmium yellow. He mixes the two unto a consistency he can stomach and then above and beyond the sad eyed lady of the post-Soviet split-lands. This phrase appeared letter after letter without premonition. First an [I] then

[I [MISS [THE
[RIGHT [STATE
[OF [MIND]

It's time to take another hit; to push this original lament from his chest like it was the Mayflower. He's planning to tax the confession wherever it settles; cheering up then catching himself, he forces gloom. No, he doesn't. It comes easy enough. Three rips and the large snap is dust; sunk into the water like his Mother eventually casts everyone from her bedroom downstairs to the couch: Her snoring husband & her adorable beanie baby/Chihuahua doggie. Maybe it was his father's vasectomy & the specter of Dodger being neutered. Maybe the pup was too feisty. She already can't sleep & This Mister can't stand to be in that house. If he was a good man he would do what he is told to do. That's what he was told.

"Then I'd have to equate good with obedience & I'm not sure they are of the same stock" he still remembers his response. He can recall so many moments vividly. He can recall instances as simple, yet relevant as standing on the steps with a hand on the banister. In the process of going to a bedroom he was given pause by his mother's stare and This Mister remembers thinking "I love how you look at me—like you look so highly of me. You look at me so long that I have to look peculiarly & say, *what*?" It's never good enough: the grades, the aptitude. This Mister is not mother's little man because she can't survive the death of their dad; no one can.

He exhales some twenty seconds later. His head collapses forward. He catches his breath and reacquaints with his senses. He stands up, perhaps which is not such a great idea so he loads a second and rips it too, small tokes he holds momentarily. He doesn't choke. He loads a small third a medium-sized snap he should be able to sink in one though it may throw him into a conniption fit.

Sure enough he rockets up like a toaster strudel and walks over to the counter by the sink where he slides the bong and the tray back to the wall.

It is time for precision not time to segue. He finishes off the coughing. He loosens the kinks in his shoulders and neck; rolling the head around. He is near the oranges and grasps for a treat. Who is it?

"Fie! It's Mel Gibson. Whatever happened to the days—the 'Man Without a Face' days?

One of THESE days?

If you don't mind I'm going to eat Maurice." He digs into the skin of Maurice with his blunt thumb presently not fitted out with an adequate nail. He forces into the fruit through and henceforth begins to peel tidbit flakes of rind from the flesh, sloppily it must be told. Juice is trailing down his fingers around his knuckles and over his palm. You could watch and be blown by the chaos inherent in deep space math. Halfway through he just tears into it—sinking his teeth, his beard is juiced. Rick Wright (the keyboardist) gets his attention when he asks This Mister *"how do you feel?"* on track three. Shivers sent through the loops and wrinkles of the brain courtesy of Vitamin C. He gnaws at it savagely, juice running across his cheeks and under his jaw towards his neck if not plummeting of the side of his face. Citrus drops to the floor. This is Maurice. This is borderline sodomy; this whole orange controversy. Its cannibalism; this is a dog eats man planet & after all is said and done it will be over. How is anyone supposed to rise above that? Really everything is within the jurisdiction of individual interpretation.

Over at the sink he rinses his hands clean. Maurice is in pieces on the floor, just like Arnie.

"Eat it!" This Mister punks his casualties then does a little wiggle over them.

While he's at it—actually after he's settled down, he brings back the monolith board propped behind the faucet. He washes his kill down with tap water one last time. He summons the corporal again to do his worst. He gets that as he grabs a paper towel nearby used to dry his hands. He wipes his mouth again. Slowly he walks back to the cutting board. Dramatically he reaches over and clasps his fingers to hold the red pepper he's lifting now to shortly set down and operate on speedily. He pulls the stem out with his thumb—numb, hollow skull beneath the vegan crown. He postulates over the pepper like a good philosopher ought before he commits sacrilege. Who in a society does the red pepper represent? If you were going to gather all of a society in a salad: the parsley would be the commoners, the mint the immigrants. The red pepper the radical: the anti-liberal, anti-everything crowd, active of course or parsley.

Very well

He slices the radical red pepper from collar to chest middle. They say if your not a faux-communist at twenty you have no heart & and if your not a republican in your mid-thirties you have no brain. Of what sort of authority are they; who to say?

He then turns the halves up, stacks them atop each other and slices along the perpendicular then splits the gathered slivers down the middle, collects and drops them on the mob blanket in the salad bowl.

Although he did not hear the telephone ring, and he's not quite sure if the ringer is on, he is cued by the beeping of his digital message device that some caller will begin talking immediately proceeding. This Mister becomes suddenly indignant as if the sanctity of his return to equilibrium has been encroached upon; violated. This Daring Caller—This Mister stands over his cutting board with a green bell; the Gore Vidal's of society. He doesn't want to see himself lashing out at the receiver because he believes everyone has abandoned him. This Daring Caller can only be satirizing, salting his earthly wounds. This Daring Caller is TWD. He said he loved This Mister & he didn't say it vindictively.

This Mister doesn't owe anybody reciprocity. He is over appealing to his sense of generosity—*for the moment, if you can't tell This Mister's floundering, I as a narrator can't help you*—isn't doing anybody, not even Juddie favors. Call him 'The Name Dropper' like 'The Decider'. 'The Name Dropper' picks up the green bell pepper and plunges ferociously into the vegetable rips out its core and pitches it against the door leaned against the wall. The seed-pellets scatter audibly across the linoleum. He supposes it's simply ironic that he pegged the banjo sporting head figure that is pointing to his heart being ejected from the opening in the instrument into a fire. Holding that thought a moment longer: he comes to reckon perhaps there is nothing simple about irony. Nevertheless his anger has been released. A profound calm comes over him. For the time being he is no longer frustrated. It's a welcome mood change, he doesn't question.

"Are you going to eat that?" one animated character asks of another animated characters heart. The animated character asked to be an organ donor has an uneasy sense of dread settling over him and expressing it self in it's posture and grimace. Just admiring Mehran's painting and breathing while the central musical theme reemerges in the middle of track three.

He returns to his station, fits the knife in then slams it through the pepper with the ferocity of a logger; so much for placid. This Mister will cut up his historians as he sees fit & to please the powers that scheme. If this Mister can't manage his emotions, how can he be expected to control who his employer happens to be? This Mister is powerless. The only power he possesses is the power to withhold his name.

The green pepper is carelessly chopped into chucks. He is stern again, the consternation, his disposition. He is unsatisfied with the quality of his new pile. He integrates the slender pepper chips over the green tabs. He then shakes his head, and after spitting some guff he avoids incising on the red pepper anymore for it is already diced well. He ends up bisecting the tabs individually, a whole medium sized pepper's worth. He knows he's thinking, even if absently, about the speaker and the message he may not have received clearly. The sensual essence he coolly rejected. He'll tell the voice leaving the message what he means. Actually if he could, he means, he'd like to but his opinions belong to him and the written page. This Mister decides that to douse hidebound minds with reasoned advice actually is the worst thing one can do in struggling to coax one from their ultimatum; or at least that's his opinion. The law is written in an undivine inventive manner.

He rinses his hands and the knife of the bell pepper seeds; washing them down the sink. This Mister may be on acid but he's prudent enough to control his population. He attains the behind the scenes key players: monastic nobility, world bankers, bones men: green onions cutting off their root ends. A soloing guitar begins its trek into the night. With the agility and perseverance of youth he slices the white ends of the green onion off. Ringlets disassemble. The inner circle at the root end becomes less insulated. Less insulated also translates to too exposed for comfort. Something apocalyptic is in the horizon. Keep a weary eye if that's all you can afford. The shadow men are dumped into the societal salad.

He pounces on the first tomato: the first guard. The he quarters, eighths and sixteenths it piling the pieces up beside him, one after the other. He cuts out the yet to be formed crowns of each Roman Praetorian guard. What's a Praetorian guardsman to do against a giant demagogue?

With the third one chopped up and the room becoming scarce for the odd structure of their stacked body parts the squishy king is brought up. His sticker is removed, alleviating him of his international renown.

With a knife into his head This Mister's sharp prodding instrument cuts around the illegitimate bastard's dome and in.

Deeper—probing into this intruder the forceful wrist turns the knife around to snatch out and off the ornamental green laurels nestled in the cranial indentation.

The plump fruit's crown is tossed into steel jaws.

They rotate as This Mister's disposal.

The king is no longer in function—split and severed. Strike that, reverse it; this regime doesn't receive a fancy funeral. Not a bullet is put to waste.

* * 9 * *

Beginning to understand the nature of things—coming to age. Innocence is willfully sacrificed for the pursuit of intrigue.

The stairs—
Where are they leading?
Why does growth occur?
It must be all the drilling!

Over lapping subjects and occurrences jumble thoughtfully during reflection. The need to arrange organizes contentions into a stature of over processed beliefs. Is that what it is all about: becoming human? Is that how we make it to heaven?

Do we have enough fuel to get there?

This Mister's still setup in the kitchen corridor; he's thinking to himself, looking down and into his soul. He puts his palm over his heart and whispers, "this is the organ which cooks my brain. I come from here. I die from here".

He dumps the tomatoes, wiping them off from the board into the tabouli becoming the salad of society's despicable caste system. He turns on the faucet to rinse off the board and knife. Simultaneously he drains his Turkish bath and bids farewell to usurpers sarcastically with an arrogant shake of the head and a sneer.

Suppose its time to sacrifice another fair and sweet—who shall it be...

Guinevere—"Sorry to wake you dear; die valiantly".

He walks over the sink cradling darling Guinevere. He sighs to feign dismay. This Mister actually couldn't be more delighted. As the fat old sun in the sky sinks beyond the horizon, This Mister make a bloody lemon of Guinevere; slicing into his palm and digging with a zeal that's a bit much. He cuts into his hand and immediately reacts, hissing with a suction which draws in all of his spit. He proceeds to slice the rind and sever the halves and then deseeds with professionally gnawing teeth. Only a tinsel of flesh is cinched between his two front teeth. Christmas comes early, this year. It must because he may not live to celebrate. He squeezes both halves ritualistically over the tabouli, rotating them clockwise in half turns to vary the grip and release more juice.

Matchsticks and staccato piano chords for harmony; in the background, a man is eating cereal, which may sound strange to some, but it is a part of the album. Another lemon is taken and split with no regard to identify he claws into her flesh—destroying her fertility symbolically. He summons the acidic liquid out her ovaries.

Little white and green ringlets start hovering or floating or pulsing.

"I'll have none of your incantations!"

Is someone hallucinating?

Of the lemons: only Ayisha remains. The horns of Shaytan; he is made to know these are and that they grow forth from the rind.

How ponderous he becomes, as This Mister cocks his head to the side, fascinated by the horns which develop splendidly. He doesn't feel ill nor does he feel at ease. He deliberates whether or not he should stomp this Jinn underfoot and add it to his catalogue of casualties. This Mister suddenly recalls sound advice from Dr. Hunter S. It is as follows: "You can turn your back to a knife, but never turn your back to a drug."

NOVEMBER 2011

Sun	Mon	Tue	Wed	Thu	Fri	Sat
		1	2	3	4	5
6	7	8	9	10	11	12
13	14	15	16	17	18	19
20	21	22	23	24	25	26
27	28	29	30			

NOTES

Estamos Chegando a Portugal em 14 dias!

This Mister backs away. What awesome powers & mystical connotations.

"Fucking green onions of society and their devil worship—I'm not above using magic!" The last part This Mister mutters vindictively—keeping his eye on Ayisha while he wraps his hand with a strip of towel.

...Huff and guff

It's quite plausible that persons will be able to recreate This Mister's dishes on account of this candid narrative. But they shall never know the secret of his pepper concoctions. They're mystical secrets. They hold illusory powers. He attains a jar with a soil-colored spice blend. He sprinkles just enough of the concoction over the salad of society's preoccupation with the dark arts. He watches with pleasure as the horns of the beast disintegrate into vapors. The final ingredient to be introduced is the cracked wheat: the essence of knowledge afloat; whose mold produces the ergot from which LSD is derived.

He measures out a ¼ cup into the measuring glass. Then he drips a handful of conjured water cupped in his hand and swishes it around twenty seconds before he jerks the cup and heaves the inflated wheat.

Toss the radio to sleep, to vision, and wake the dream...of course it was tap water—don't get it twisted.

He actually improvises the interpolating phrases to accompany Allen who in the background of the Pink Floyd's performance is enjoying his jazz-infused psychedelic breakfast for some time before the band wraps.

A little bit of olive oil: laurels are all This Mister's salad of society's hardships needs. Not too much, more like hardly any. This Mister doesn't wish to endow his mock society with the confidence to develop the sense of smell and sniff out his tyranny. This Mister is quite prudent and understands what *almost* all of his actions mean. He knew his appetizer was missing something.

He grabs two large silver serving spoons from the top drawer. This Mister mixes rhythmically—lifting the contents of his bowl from the sides and unearthing the buried; giving it rise. He plunges into the salad, and it all becomes one. The ingredients are summoned from the bottom and they fall atop the mixture and the prejudice is disavowed. It is stated in multiple and different ways because of the repetition necessary to thoroughly mix his society prone to isolationist tendencies. Now he returns the tired tabouli in the refrigerator to rest after a brief yet intense outing. It is here he catches the chicken hiding. He brings it out and sets the thighs on the counter.

He realizes he wouldn't dare eat all six, so he'll just pick up three. This Mister couldn't consume such a quantity. It doesn't matter however; this it is to be a feast. And This Mister is expecting company in the form of spirits. There is no second place. This Mister is well aware that leaving food out for spirits is akin to leaving cookies for Papa Noël. It's the Zen Buddhist in him.

This Mister runs full the water and washes them all off anyway; silently choosing which three to cut while he handles. It's reminiscent of the grade school, or the street-court would-be jock cuts. This Mister chooses players which are going to bolster the image of his team.

"Image finances" This Mister boasts with the candor of a made man.

In the cupboard directly above the stovetop is more yellow Tupperware. It's smaller, similar, for as much as it matters. He ornamentally presents the dish on the much less crowded countertop all the lemons once made their stoop. Then he turns to face the doorless frame of the pantry and retrieves a Cajun pepper concoction in a small squared Tupperware container with lid. This Mister sprinkles some of the rub in the bowl. He also pours in some salt and sifts flour from a bag over at last before he swishes the bowl around. This Mister makes these preparations for the chicken thighs that shall be swished around & then sit like a crowd of beach bums rubbing on the seasoning and barking at the lack of ladies breezing by these pseudo-studs.

From the pantry he retrieves a bag of rice. Returning he stirs up the lentils in the dish in which the rice will soon rise. He measures one cup of rice in a dry measuring cup and pours it in. Now it's time finally for the hot surface units. He turns the back right burner back on. Next he pulls out a pot and pours a lake of oil into it—just enough to coat the surface area and turns on the flame beneath.

This Mister employs his prerogative to breathe. Once the oil is hot, but before it begins to smoke he turns the burner down to medium heat and adds the chicken thighs. They need to cook six to eight minutes on each side. It's a good time to stoke the appetite with a toke or two from his pipe. This Mister finds his pipe on a stout bookshelf by his rocking chair on the other side of the partition. He pinches a popcorn nugget from the tray on the table and smokes standing. It occurs to him that he hasn't written but one line all night long. This Mister is able to shrug that off. He knows phrases are anxious as plankton in the suction of a humpback whale.

Six to eight minutes pass in and out of trance, watching the boiling oil scald the chicken thighs. He drops in one bay leaf from the jar on the ledge before him. Then This Mister adds 75% of the onions from the refrigerator. He must keep a watchful eye on the onions. The slices of pungent bulb begin to melt with their due irritation. He stirs the onions at length to loosen all adhesive tendencies.

This Mister is ready to finish preparing this dinner even though it'll be another half hour at least. All dishes should be done at the same time the mujudura is on low & his timings are right. On his umpteenth trip to the pantry, he brings forth a celebrated mist: the cumin, which is blessed upon the starch dish known by the native creators as mujudura. He puts a lid on it. The onions are squealing slivers like children, they require constant attention.

He gets a frying pan out of the drawer. Grabbing it by its ring, he unfolds the handle bringing it from a compacted position. He repossesses the oil and pours a small puddle then brushes it out with a wad of towel to coat the entire surface. This Mister adds the onions he didn't use before in the new pan. He bisects the slivers haphazardly while they remain in the dish with the paring knife once more prior to their transfer. He now has more infantilism to deal with.

He stops everything, and walks away to get a drink, rubbing it between his parched lips. Juice slips easily down his metallic tongue or storm drain. He really hasn't stopped a thing, it's just an expression. He washes the seasoning dish out to be used again—peculiar how the lid looks atop the mujudura he notices in grabbing the Tupperware. It is not a match, crowning the small pot. The royal headgear is much too cumbersome atop the head of regentless head of state. He tends his flocks then tickles the young lord's brains. To compliment the chicken dish fancifully he grabs a casket of mushrooms but just sets it down then proceeds to open the can of corn, from on the counter set previously. For some reason, the brand of corn he purchased, at wholesale cost, has a holding slop rather thick and peculiar. It is on the verge of disgusting him. He dumps almost half of the slop into the Tupperware reluctantly until he cannot stand to be paralyzed by its horrific quality anymore so he disposes of the remainder, something his mother would not allow however she is not here nor is she equipped with an Atom Heart by the way. If he was a good man he'd make no mention. Alas he has and is not sorry, merely pathetic.

Stirring it out with the same wooden spoon in silence he watches over the onions for a few moments and packs another bowl. From the tray of fungus, he only obtains a deuce, and fractions them one at a time. Remembering that he forgot to save some bell pepper, he picks some of the green out of the tabouli and relocates it; adding it directly into the chicken now smothered in onions. The mushrooms he dumps into the Tupperware dish with the corn accident. The sloth will probably cook out of the corn or it's not bad. He tastes it. Did he purchase cream of corn by mistake? No, This Mister purchased whole kernel corn. Damn! The corn was supposed to replace the peas. Oh well, it's not like he's cooking a whole fryer. There will be enough corn to go around.

Two cut vanish; he slices up some more mushrooms. Progressively he cuts down ideas and speculated reasons. This is the work of his rationale, more appropriately his rationalizing ego which makes way for id to frolic. Like forests the time has come with emerging urgency to scamper again and get lost. Once he's lost count of the amount he's procured he stops, scrapes up his cleanest pile, and stirs the pot up again. He's then to walk away a while and let the children spoil, rather than spoil the children. It's a simple lesson: shock them. The seasoned king, wiser already, is sucking up the water of his follies, and is a much fuller shade of distinguished, pardoned, and decent, a Platonic philosopher-king—well maybe that's an overstatement & actually, This Mister needs to do some more seasoning. He grabs paprika, lemon pepper, cayenne pepper for the smothered chicken, lemon grass, and salt from the pantry. He knows the mujudura has a tendency of coming out dry so he seasons his sautéed onions with paprika, salt, lemongrass, lemon pepper, and he doubles back for a pinch of thyme. Does he know what he's doing? Not exactly, but they all compliment relatively. He samples an onion sliver once he's stirred it around. It has a full, peppered-herb flavor. Lastly he measures out about ½ teaspoon of salt and ¼ of cayenne. Now he can turn the burner down on the frying pan and devote his attention elsewhere.

A bag with a pair of bread loafs is summoned from somewhere. Apparently it has been present just inconspicuous all this time, as some persons are capable of sticking around without gathering overwhelming notice. They manage not to be voted out as do some of America's shakers & movers. Just like almost every History Channel program makes some mention of Adolph Hitler, no contemporary work of American literature is complete without it's Bush's Brain—allusion to MC Rove.

There really is nowhere to go. The only thing to do is sell your self short.

This Mister may be dreaming, but he's not asleep.

He breaks out half of the chosen loaf and slices it down the breadth with The General: a long serrated knife with prongs. Steam from the chicken stew rises. He keeps the broken quarters. He has made two cuts—neither kosher. He returns the rest of the loaf into its plastic sack. Grabbing at the butter on it's shelf in the refrigerator door, he thinks better and heads for the unwrapped cube on a small saucer in the pantry.

He resists the waxed mutants smothering his thighs. They are no longer alone or at the bottom, because he just lifted them to worm over and actually smother as the dish calls for. He lets the dish simmer, turns down the heat and finds a cover that fits. But before he caps it, he adds just 1/6 cup of water. He will stir occasionally until the chicken is tender. Then add his corn and mushrooms hold the peas.

"I should have done green beans" there is no next time, but This Mister does not endure dismay after what he's said.

The diced onions are brown and syrupy. He pours them over the mujudura and returns the crown respectfully. He butters the bread, from the warm melting cube, not in lather but with mind to abstain. He adds garlic powder, and onion powder. He sticks the bread in the oven on the wire racks, no tray and then quickly sweeps through the scene.

This Mister takes a much needed rest from the rigors of cooking his best. He sits down at the table. He picks up his ½ ounce sack of stress bud and pulls out a few spade nugs. He proceeds to break them up, twisting them from their stem ripping the plant to shreds. Occasionally a seed will pop out woven into the center of each spade. He takes his yield and crushes it lifting portions and creating friction through forceful handling. He next searches the table around for a pack of rolling leaves. Not finding one, he heads over to into the living room towards the drafting table.

It's all dark and he almost swoons in the atmosphere of his den. How conspicuous! The zigzags are placed in plain sight near the head of the table hugging a tin can that holds all his pens. He opens the flap to the package of rolling papers and pulls one out between his fingers. Fingering it around he ends up pinching a cut-corner of it its otherwise flimsy nature; he flexes it like a board, providing minimal support. He picks up his allotted amount and sprinkles it across the length of the leaf as evenly as possible. With the carton of rolling papers he scrapes the remaining dust off the front edge of the table where his open tray awaits. Now with two hands he begins to roll the marijuana together in its wrapper gathering density. He works the lump down in the center. He gradually brings the front of the paper down so that he can quickly tuck it under and roll it over. Like it closed? Lick it and then shake it solid holding a flap and twisting an end.

He picks up his lighter and lights the twisted end, blowing, allowing it to sizzle down. He puts the joint in his mouth and lights it smack puffing on it to keep it lit. He continues to give it spark separated by short intervals desiring to keep the hooter cherried.

Is there a top to this staircase? Most men must barter to acquire enough hope to believe so. Can a lone trekker expect this obstacle to bring him to anything other than death should he/she attempt to scale? Should he perish? What then, if This Mister was to reach the top of one the set only to find another, steeper, longer case? What is the worth of elevating by stations? And if the above is the case, what of the other respect: descent? What if subconscious has a subconscious, and we are really digging deeper into an abyss instead of climbing into the light? And is it possible to exactly define whether this case one takes is to ascend or, descend?

Aren't we frozen, that is still in life to begin with, bound to place? Never mind.

Words are always relative symbols. Adjectives decorate figures of the imagination.

Opinions have no cornerstone and can be shattered by disbelief.

The virtual

The appearance of the stairs can change. Cloud formations in head will re-associate automatically. No matter the appearance, all one has to do is consciously attempt to expand or move their player away from their origin. It's not a game.

Whatever—person then
Later on
Find yourself retuning

* * 10 * *

Fade in on a man exposed. His legs stretched out, relaxing, exhaling the smoke that really aggravates his brain. He could bang his skull against Mehran's piece for almost the same effect. It's nice.

He consistently drags the joint, sinking down into the chair as if his body was blending with the leather. In a hand gesture with a certain *Je ne sais quo* he searches for a thought, needing the ability to strictly compose, he retrieves from a pocket his miniature graphite-cover poem book.

It's good to just think, to think about going through with the imperative. He keeps smoking, he stops worrying, but he still deciphers. He coughs a spell. In front of him the thick bellowing smoke spirals while the walls breathe and purple hazy visions wave and weave a tapestry before him. There is no more This Mister brown eyes. His pupils likely consume the whole iris. He lifts himself up in his chair. He opens the flap to his notebook and slowly looks past his writings and pen drawings. He fumbles for a digit in his pocket and pulls out a measly green oil pastel.

Intimately he scribbles in a word, with the proper adjustment of the eyes. Faintly it states: [proverb]. He rubs it out. It's still slightly visible through the smudge. Ash falls onto his lap. He wipes it off. He starts to draw below. He rips down the paper surrounding the balled tip of his crayon.

Smoking he has another look around in the room, honing in on interest.

He takes a few more hits to the face, before he stands up and roams around. He puts the joint down on the toaster-oven near him, its cherry hanging off; just the resonated roach left.

"I'm just going to leave it, or the heat will escape" This Mister says, referring to the crowned regent, before he reclaims his still-cherried roach. He looks out the wall because he doesn't have a kitchen window.

Adolescence is the springtime This Mister loathes. The continually surfacing epiphanies of what life is, are ruining his contentions. As you age opportunity is replaced by experience & memories...and regret. It is evening and he is an emotional wreck. It's wrong to wallow inside during the era of promise and squander this, the most precious of all precious resources: youth. To have the wailing sounds agitating his head and pulsating in his inner ear instead. Other people just tell him to be steadfast and that at least he's not in Iraq. Why do frightful voices, vices, views outnumber the patriotic assemblies? Is there no room for comfortable breathing tactics? Will we cease to find pleasure in the harmony of the simple natured excavator? Where is the secret to humanity; held in the eye of the torchbearer, or in the hand of the First Mover? Who bears the torch by the way? Does humility make you humble? Is every famine virtual? Can we be humble much longer or does the inner demon egg exfoliate and interact with the hands that keep the time to the clock? Fate is complex.

He has yet to turn the broiler on & he will abstain still.

It could be twenty minutes longer that he will have to wait. It's time to or he feels like reading poetry—no, dreaming. This Mister feels like projecting into chapters beyond this time in his life. What would they be like, if he were to survive tonight?

To attempt this in mind, This Mister closes his eyes...

* * 19 * *

He's a frosted flake, soggy in the fish bowl. In the future he's running from his past. It's like evading John Medeski in *tonic* hallways, tumbling forever.

There's red ground behind the pasted illustrations. In colored markers gawking faces are frozen about looking at the representation they happen to be amongst. Six dollars for eacho Veggies: your ebony coat, the finest brother. I didn't know, I can't explain...how do your caricatures hover and orbit?

Mehran heard something like death in the screams of his predecessors. He captured it on this door as prophecy of our doom; humbly dedicating it.

Educate us on death by chemical extermination, are we just roaches? Driven by cock No how ugh!! Is it true? "Not now John," barked Roger Waters. "Doesn't this bother you?"

* * 20 * *

Sue or cede to hide it is. Sue or cede to hide they call it: the sequel.

* * 21 * *

The mob lingers around to be choked from the score. Then chopped up MORE! Draped dismembered to the floor in unison, no on fours, shame. What's next? A course, of course, the appetizer has been served. The entrée: soon.

* * 22 * *

Chapter twenty-two bring god spells.

With only seconds remaining, solitary and unstrung: once the graphics before you are removed you are left with what you create. There's a white scheme with no dimension.

* * 23 * *

Let us move presently into the evils distressing this being, hopefully. Ha, you know how that is *anxious* plankton blown in the ocean. Hope and/or evils; answers, the nature of being, the likelihood of clarification. They are all swaying and/or in freefall. So adopt the parlance of the East Coast and *forget about it.*

* * 24 * *

Let us talk about the future streaming by rapidly.

Chapter twenty-five would be lovely this e*va*ning. Girl, I'm so unnerved chasing you.

* * 25 * *

Sit, He is already. *Alone?* But? *Eva's not coming.* But? That's the way it is. How thrilled will This Mister be? He is true to life, a blue grape there's no time for: just like guilt in a way: unbelievable as all these colons.

Incidentally:: We think we are dissecting the truth when we pose on the steps and talk in chains of progressing thought. We refine all the things we know for the daily notice paid. Resign by visual prowess to commemorate. The wrinkles in our brain are the substance of our imagination. Enlightenment would be rendering the individual being led from its vestal bliss into the subconscious worlds of Id to love and loathe life altogether and emerge as this forlorn character: a dead mameluk: whole

* * 26 * *

Galloping along the story. He's half-dead, tired of dreaming of red Corgan at the stop sign. Billy you hurt some adored-one upsetting vocalizations chastising.

This is changing. I feel something touching, can he? Here's how it goes.

* * 27 * *

This is going to seem like the longest chapter. Wait until twenty-eight, until your children play with scapegoats in Tom Wait's corridor Mule, you vigilante. What's happening? You better handle this page.

A new character, signaling with hands is only too glad to can (as in condemn/trash). It is rendered as a pawn (as in insignificant) with the upper-torso of a man. Rounded out just below his belly is a banjo. Flowing from his open sound hole beating still the blood belly is exiled into the three-dimensional realm where it encounters the wastebasket with virtual ease. The waste basket: obscured of course by the man in the leather chairs, who is so pleased to hear you, they are older than you think darling.

Don't let someone else tell you that: Caution: colons.

* * 28 * *

Now since the organ knows it'll be received as garbage, it can settle down. This organ follows its trajectory. Wandering imagination successively travels. Towards the disposal of what is passed off for guards to handle. This is the familiar ground. Remind him to forget all that's around only to excite, later. Now...okay, later.

Incompatible it takes to flight, sexually shying away. Secrecy does not accommodate. What is this becoming? His life story? How's it go so far?

* * 29 * *

Fantasy cannot fulfill; death. Smashing the sacrilegious; death gets its fill of life. Confounded fanatic cannot fulfill as envisioned theistically. He will try. He will try to pity. He will have been known as the great dealer of remorse.

Scattered and dissipating: onto the dark side: he goes. He's been. He went. Here he is with a viola; tuned by a player.

Here he is smoked like a chamber. Extinguished flame of the Bunsen burner yearns. Have twenty more one mores & end up with the math correct at least for sake of sporting the fast times while they're killing you. You need sleep.

* * 30 * *

An entire rug.
You're stuck with quilting. Come back next year.

Though *by the way*
Weren't the twenties roarin'?

* * 33 * *

Um yea can I get a pump fake, yeah: the jukes? Hash browns & mustard @ Mc Donald's coming down…Wal-Mart manual pads…

* * 34 * *

Errors like chapters thirty-one and thirty-two are cancelled out of their allotted space because This Transient Being is too busy quilting to get to lively.

* * 35 * *

Not like with flint a spark could settle but try me. I'm funny. I'm going to finish a book in a chapter, wanna read? Fantastic for you, if you: turn the page.

It might hurt to please you.

* * 10 AGAIN * *

This Mister wakes up and looks around. The roach is burnt out between his fingers; he flicks it to the table. He sits straight, hunched. He squints and scrutinizes as he scans the living room. If he could read the inside of his eyelids without, it's hard to say, writing over them with bold new dream schemes. if he could read the back of his eyelids he could review the virtual pastures traversed. He fills his cheeks and pumps the air out through the funnel of his slightly parted lips. His eyebrows rise up to that line on the forehead people usually say they're up to when they have been nearly fed full of a person's actions or general demeanor…It feels like ten o' clock. Can it be that late? He springs up. More importantly, did he burn anything? He lifts the lid on the smothered chicken. The aroma is profound.

"Perfect."

Quickly This Mister adds the mushrooms and corn then returns the lid.

"6 minutes."

This Mister is confident. He turns the burner under the mujudura off & turns the broiler on. He stoops over and peers through the slit & tsks.

The garlic bread clashes with his ensemble. Really he can't use—he decides to put it in the fridge, buttered and seasoned. He retrieves one pita pocket instead and flings it onto the top oven rack. It's a steep angle but This Mister knows how to get it through; just fling it gently and it won't fall, it will crash land and stop.

He sets an obtained dinner plate down. Its blue border is decorated with spirals around. Next he attains a platter which does not match his dinner plate. He spreads the mujudura over in a cake and sets it on the counter. He brings the salad bowl and the pitcher to the table. He fills his glass and then returns the pitcher. He returns the paint tubes to the basket and pushes it and the jar of brushes to the side. He examines his hands. There's oil on the side of a few fingers and the butt of his left hand but remarkably not on his palms or tips of fingers. He requisitions a moment for relief. This Mister just tries to be a professional, or at least have some standards and not paint over nature's colorful bounty; out of respect for Mother Earth and the I and I of course.

So…the eek passes.

He does the smart thing and turns the red light off. Then he walks in the dark to the fridge; blind spot again. He drinks from the cold crystal jug to exhilarate his mirth with water. As a tribute to God's staple creations: fire-music-math his hands back off from the glass jug he's lifted overhead before to commemorate. Shards scatter across the floor following the explosion of. the jug. Forensics could examine the evidence using math and tell exactly how the collision scattered the debris. The splashing water may have been enough to put out a fire depending. The brilliance of the satellite is closed away. Everything, except his appreciation of fine music can be banished from his heart.

He returns to the table now and as he nears a light switch he flips up to illuminate the area over his soon to be seated self. The chandelier provides near pure light so that while he eats his food can be seen clearly and his imagination hopefully shall not lead him to wildly predict, and fear his food is infested. Around the table he sits down.

Not instantly, but before he drifts into a spell he realizes he's missing several things. He looks up at the platter.

"Perfect. Six minutes." Everything seems fine.

He rises and maneuvers from his seat, turns off the stove units, opens and then reaches into the oven with the same hand he has wrapped in a hand towel to grab the pita which he couldn't tell you by anymore than intelligent reasoning whether it was hot or not, because his hand was so insulated. He leaves the oven open and couriers the pocket bread to the table toute suite.

His chicken smothered in onions courtesy of Mr. Bam! Lagasse looks magnifique. Everything Lebanese he learned from watching and his Aunt Terry. Everybody's got an aunt or a godparent in the family who does all the ethnic cuisine and in some cases for her entire church or community God willing. She can just be in the kitchen all day and neat.

The mound of lentils and rice is a fine foundation for the main course. Unfortunately there is no further need for his wooden security instrument. He pinches it between the oven door and its upper lip and then sits down calmer than you are.

* * 11 * *

He rises once more to collect for himself some silverware: a fork and those two serving spoons. Upon sitting he serves himself a portion of the rice bed, balancing a chicken thigh and splitting it in half as he serves.

"Hmm, the chicken is tender". He scoops atop this thigh its smothering onions amongst other accoutrements to congest his inhalation. He mixes the salad of society's labors a spell and with his crane he attains, swings the load over his plate and wins it. He rips a corner of bread leaving the rest on the serving plate.

Holding half a wing of bread he takes his first bite, leading with the fork. This Mister stabs for a piece some smothered poultry. He chews and the juices flood his palette. How do you say tasty in body language: with slightly up turned lips, a subtle bob; a nod of This Mister's head?

Bits cling on his porch and are swept inside by digits from the face and lip area. The light casts brightness over his table. The illumination is glorious. This is a special supper. There are several reasons why he didn't invite anybody even though This Mister cooked for three. In all honesty This Mister is expecting an apparition or two to show.

This Mister fills his pita roll with mujudura and chicken next. His pita face is stuffed and his lips protrude with an air of the primate. He manages to chew the mujudura and the chicken he may have caught unless it is a spoiled enfant; you know a fried onion.

The majority of everything remains uneaten. He's not stalling, This Mister is just making the moment last by sweet talking time. He grabs his book and pastel nearest and scribbles down something private. He scoops some tabouli in his bread craft and revels in the zest of the lemon and the juiciness of the red bell pepper in particular. This Mister sets up a mix with chunk of chicken. Juices and goop run off. For some reason he thinks of a pair of legs running from knives and finds he has no sympathy to charitably contribute. The difficulty of chewing; his cadence is adagio until he stops in disgust. The king of evil looks, cheeks full like burrowing squirrels that ran awry. He scrapes like a razorblade playing with the locks on a suitcase. In this case it's his fork scraping the plate; dissecting the corn, doing the work of an emulsifier. In silent seclusion, spiritually disavowed; his sentence is to loathe the land. His father absent around the table does not do much to sundry the downpour. Perhaps upstairs father is preparing kindling in his bed for him to burn.

Slowly, steadily, he sits back and sets the fork to rest. He picks up slowly, to close his grip around the cup and lift to it his lips so he can sip to quench. This Mister performs the gesture with the most deliberate air. He must be so deep in thought he is weary of having an accident. Fulfilled he sets down his cup, slowly, cautiously. It gets closer, tipping down onto the surface as a reluctant but reassured toe. The whole bottom becomes flush. He does not come to letting go. He reaches a new depth in the tide of thirst. Vanquished it seems, he gulps more before he reassembles his posture around the dinner arrangement.

With his fingers and cupped bread he forks some of the substance smothering the chicken without the thick fried flesh over some of the mujudura in his bread boat and sails it comfortably into his open mouth.

He bites into rather than sinking the boat whole. He eats sushi, he really should know better. Now gunk spills out the back and from the sides of the vessel. Lentils base-jump from his mouth.

This Mister is just thinking how meaty the meat is and that's it's rather disgusting him because it's so thick to chew through when he notices—

"What up Kafka?"

"The Meat? Aww…It's the LS4. The chicken isn't sitting well in my stomach."

"Shall I fix you a plate?"

His holographic guest declines, and tells him there's no need for the Zen Buddhist. This Mister suddenly feels overtly stuffed. Perhaps he's disgusted by the crude appearance of his hybrid dung beetle guest dripping mucilaginous. Decides it's enough. Scribbles a command to a servant on the adjoining page, directed at the face he drew adjoining. The Kafka Bug peers over as if he's worried This Mister is writing something compromising about it.

This Mister lifts his head and has that strained smile powered by the coyness people exhibit at their employer, ex, despised parents/guardians, mechanics et al. "They never did figure out what you really were, throughout that commentary and supplementary analysis as long as or longer than your exposition." Because that's a rough way to break the ice he rapidly follows up, "You didn't invite Kant. Or am I inappropriate? What of Aristophanes? I need to quell this love like disease." Somebody's assumed the role of antagonist.

The Kafka Bug sits back in its seat. Its little insect arm resting on the ridge; Kafka Bug is just digging this Mr. Obliviot.

There are a few moments of silence.

"So…"

This Mister stabs some flesh and gives it his second opinion. ghla! He gags and spits it out in his lap. Never mind his manners—where are his paper towels when he needs a napkin.

For the doters: that is minding his manners.

This Mister is preoccupied for a while picking the shred of chicken off his crotch and focusing on the stain it has left. When he looks up The Kafka Bug is gone.

"Ya' probably got lost in your own stage directions! A'ight then."

Staring at the plate, he picks it off the table and walks it over to the sink. His plate is nearly clean. He just scraped it off onto the serving platter. He'll quickly toss the dishes in the fridge; but not literally. Isn't the anticipation usually better than the event? He leaves a piece of bread out near the open flap of his notebook in event of catatonic hunger, or disaster.

Next he decides to spend a few moments watching his step after he's delivered the dishes to the storage compartment. He deliberately pressures his feet atop the large glass chunks to crush them. He balances over some large convex shards and spins in a circle before they shatter under the force he commands.

Pastels, marijuana, rolling papers, and paint: these are a few of his favorite things. All the dirty dishes are stacked in the sink. With no care, hands away from the hot stovetop, he pops pieces of glass and smashes them to splinters with the heel of his foot. Spinning and falling off of axis on a large concaved fragment he catches himself over the sink luckily. Inspects his palms and phew, he continues interested with his placid maneuvers until he finishes his interpretative maneuvers upon shards of fused sand particles.

With all his paints and palette gathered, This Mister discards the used towels and nabs a few new before he leaves the kitchen for the den. He hops atop his desk. Meanings at this point escape him: the meaning to puzzles, of clearly formative events and instances, his harbored contentions, his raw reactions, fear, and assertiveness. He prefers it that way. His reluctance can be deceiving; his resolve however will be indisputable. He may stall until he's bored and then that is when he'll make an unconscious move. Realizing is not the folly, it is evidently clear he meant to be at the mercy of the wind. When Hunter S. Thompson checked out, the taste of the breeze and the shade provided by the trees and the heroism of thieves changed dramatically. This Mister became keenly aware of the Great American Sleep that has descended over the suburban landscape especially. The only refuge of the disenfranchised and societies scoundrels is to choose the time they bid adieu. He perfectly understands. There is no empathy necessary. It's futile to be cynical and fatal to be involved. That cannon, that one hundred-fifty foot cannon which shot the capsule containing the ashes of Dr. Hunter S. Thompson signaled something terrible. It provided This Mister with a whole new initiative that was dangerous and irresistible; frightening but not foreign. Then he instantly felt that he had so much too live for.; not enough memories. Still it's the business. Concerned dread connected with taking over the family business in the absence of the sole-proprietor, the sole-benefactor, Daddy, looms like trenches.

What is the meaning? In the hour of death does it become all too relevant?

Why should it, life won't matter; he picks up his viridian green and vermilion red. They are fancy names for ivy green and a fire orange relatively. With the viridian he applies the paint heavily in a rectangular strip; taller than wide however the width of this strip is substantial. It is at least a foot wide, left of the desks center. Traveling with vertical strokes is like shading templates with a crayon. The paint does not lay flat over the textured wall. Characters and eventually a scene develop from the shapes. It feels archeological, like uncovering some, hopefully, tumultuous exchange.

Beside this stripe, right of center This Mister now paints the shade of red described as fire orange. This vermilion hue applied blankets and reveals with the same vigor as the color opposing. Perhaps there shall be a war of the colors & their inherent energies. Perhaps it shall be a war where vegetation is pitted against the all-consuming flame. It seems as predictable as the war that pits white against black; but there are bound to be upsets and surprises worth tuning into. He needs some tension. He just sits their transfixed. It's more dynamic than watching a Chia pet grow grass.

Speaking of grass…

This Mister gets off to check on his resonated roach. Besides he needs to let the paint dry before he does what he thinks he wants to next. He finds it on the table and stands there back in the kitchen in the soft incandescent light sparking a Bic and looking over the kitchen a while and his piece near Mehran's. He's not tripping, nor is he Joshing. This Mister actually spread oil paint all over these apartment walls.

"There's paint all over the carpet, they would've painted the walls anyways."

At this point, if it's contrived and seems deliberate it must be logic—more precisely, what logic has resigned it self to measure & produce.

He rescues himself from a stupor, with his eyes fixed on the spoon getting charred set in the crevice door as if it were alabaster. The paint is not too thick he decides to venture back. He adds more of the vermillion red to his brush and paints a C, like a half-circle near the top on the left side just up to the centerline. He then wipes the red all the way off his brush onto a towel. On the other side he does the exact opposite with viridian green over the vermillion backdrop, a backwards C, the other half of the circle. At the point where a horizontal line would pass through the right side of the circle he paints a tangent line bending down into the center some ways below.

Ivy of course over the fire orange; This Mister renders a complete nine (9).

Nine (9): the number endowed with such a mystique. It is not a prime number like seven (7). It is square like four but not an even divide (4). It is daunting, speaks to the inherent discord; of the uneven distribution of wealth & resources & opportunity. He shakes his head before it with puckered, outturned lips like an ape and proclaims, "It's beyond me."

Then This Mister starts clapping syllables. He claps thirt-y-three-deg-rees. He claps num-er-ol-o-gy. Coincidence? Toying with the limited intellectual capacity of the one rebellious fiery Prince of jinn; who is he? Iblis.

This Mister—not he to which allusions are made, grows silent and pensive. Then he seems on the verge of dictating something poetic to appeal to our emotions in a charming way at least once in the course of this turbulent and erratic onslaught.

He dedicates, streaming, "Love is the nine/the meaning of life//In the course/someone will always give/suffer/endure more//Love is the truth/how I adore these sad truths//We run from love/we've spat at lovers//Still love is constant/don't neglect//Like I've forgotten/to be a child"

Wiping the brush away he reapplies some viridian and paints a silly line from the base across the dividing line. It is squiggly symbolizing an awry life path/style: a dizzy adventure of culpable misfortune. This adventure may make the painting look ugly because he, in a confused anguish scoots himself away.

* * 12 * *

This Mister kneels besides his computer as if he were going to confide some close-guarded secret at it. Instead he pushes a button to eject the tray: picture of a cow lolling in the grass. He'd rather cast his gaze down and away than address any more issues at the moment, perhaps for the rest of the day.

Turn over the essence of Pendulum Master who lays down the challenges for the excursing. There is always a way around an obstacle. There bloody well is a sure shot to the lonely top. It's like playing the stocks in respects to the risk involved & the depravity eminent. Losses are appreciably greater than the cost of the ticket, than the sum you can get for your soul.

When they say you can always leave that quick shot success to the cockpit, they are right, yet they are ignorant. They are unaware of another's sick sense: the sense of emotional belonging. Humans develop dependencies to anything and everything that gives them the chance.

How easy is it to detach human desire from the radiant specter of the bliss on the other side? How easy is it to detach human desire from impressive riches in mind, soul, wealth, function, and status, & sex? How easy is it to call a mirage's bluff? Instead we strap ourselves to fickle institutions which could give away any time and land us back into the dugout; or worse yet onto the DL. The danger is none the less exhilarating. Where are the negative attributions?

Light searching the outer fields finds a man in a chair, rocking slowly, tying his locks. He has come to realize, just now, that he is a thorn in the crown of the messiah. This is why he must remove his spike from the temple of the Son of Man.

He sits there a long time pondering his actions: diffracting them, trying to tune into a station he hasn't permeated to anticipate a new point of view. He rocks in a loose but rhythmic formation in the quiet. He has put Atom-Heart-Mother away.

The rocking of his feet; heel-forward, toe-back is continuous and he continues with his hand, the right one through his hair. His facial hair becomes thick mostly beneath his chin, down the arch of his neck. He lays his hand flat down to feel around with his fingertips the prickle buds on his cheeks of the premature beard he cannot yet grow.

Long distant flashing red eyes search the spaces for time portals and past emotions that can be nostalgically restored for beneficiary contemplation. His throat is somewhat irritated. He's waiting patiently for the poisonous nature of natural gas to fill this compartment and put an end to these footnotes on a winter's tale. Is this a shortness of breath he's feeling? No, but it's a need to cough. Poison in the mind for real—for real, for real.

"Poise son with the green apple on the paper cloth." This Mister uttered nothing of the sort.

"What?" He replies in fright. He leans forward and turns on his vision box set. Let it be known This Mister is crazy enough to not subscribe to cable TV. He doesn't even have thirteen channels to call shit and complain of the lack and/or lackluster of what he has to choose from. He doesn't even receive one channel so he turns it up the snow so that the static is audible and drowns out the haunting quiet. Slowly he treads back to his seat and with both hands working side by side around the modulated portion of the skull he begins flexing his hair bent and straight desiring to wrap it up or do something that is absolutely nothing now.

He perceives a lone lighthouse in a sea of interference where scrambled messages struggle to tread in the foreground and register in his head. His boyish nobility (naivety) and ignorance is locked away somewhere in that lighthouse. This Mister thinks he ought to just abandon it altogether. The pretentious dream schemes are not portentous. The ominous are the simple truths such as: it's destructive to fall in love. To procure love is another story entirely.

Even good people are capable of great evil. That is, to come of Sarah, plain & tall with regurgitated homespun notions about the world and all therein.

Tying up his dreadlocks one on the side and in the back; what's he looking at? He's looking at something outside past the bicycle, through the glass door, maybe even through the fence, through each and every edifice through the city, across the country across the oceans, in the ether. This Mister leans forward and peers. He's shaky & disheveled, standing and creeping hunched over; his blue-black rectangle pattern boxers visible as well as the tiny valley before the split into cheeks. Vertebrae distinguished through his clinging Tee, the narrator at his back—ready to stab?

Below the waist line thread ties to his pants pocket, over the tear, a patch with symbolizes his Lebanese ethnicity. This Mister endures the sudden mental flash which brings his father back. He is lying face down on hardwood; dead & dying sometime in the night, sometime in the fourteenth year of his shattered life since then. Drool is pooling around his reactionless lips and clinging to his puffy cheeks. That shattered adolescent had a friend to see off at four in the morning and a paper route to throw. For sure he breaks down when he returns though to a blanket draped over his father's body, nay corpse. Anyways, in brief timeless moments of meditation he can hug him on a plateau overlooking the hills, admiring the way they roll and the many fluorescent colors of the sunset from the grassy knoll where no shots are fired...

Crazy sometimes to save the life
To whom it may concern: apologies. This Mister is intent on dropping the curtain on this private affair shortly. Regret will vanish instantly when the world is rid of This Mister who sells himself down the river rather than sailing upstream on his box spring. He'd dream of mercy in the street, of meeting Peter Gabriel consoling Anne Sexton compassionately—if it were up to him. In the humdrum he hears his soul singing and wishes his daddy still could take him into his arms. This is widely known by now: the guardian and discipline issues. This Mister feels like an orphan and is pretty sure this world doesn't need another prophet.

* * 13 * *

Coming up from his knees, he walks over to the PC tower with a new saucer to command, sets the program then wanders out of sight into the kitchen for the tray he left the broken green shake on. He sits down with it on the rocking chair and removes the pipe from his pocket, then sets the tray beside him, on an altar. He lights the sun yellow and fireball fuchsia flames and the altar takes on its own life. Behind this display on the wall: the memorable Pink Floyd pin up from the 1969 "Ummagumma" release: the enlarged pictograph of the cover of the studio album. Below it on the altar's stage as well is a large glass bottle, and the Gigi vinyl album cover to demonstrate true devotion an appreciation of The Pink Floyd's sonic art. He's replicated a portion of the set for the picture of the band sequentially in and outside; you'd have to be familiar.

The composition he is listening to happens to be track five, the title track from "A Saucerful of Secrets" the previous LP, released as the band was leaving their founder Syd behind, whose incoherence was becoming a hindrance. 'A Saucerful of Secrets' is a long psychotic composition in all its stages like the LSD trips they enthralled. It starts out soft and enchanting; ricocheting chimes and ever growing organ chords open. He's packed a stiff bowl. As the synthesized sounds enter the program the curious mood is gradually replaced by the somber tones. He finds himself in a forest atmosphere still and eerie.

He is buckling in his chair and coughing. Rocking, the whining chair creaks. He lifts his pipe back up to his mouth to toke. The pitched sounds are dialed into the upper registers. The echoes and chaotic arrangement are perfectly produced and controlled to be ever so hypnotic. There are several species of whiners, screeching demons that find their way on sonar fixes through the night. Removing his finger once from the carb, then a second and third time in a quick open-close pattern it happens: the smoke from the chamber is brought into his lungs. The synthesized noise patterns desensitize his mind; he looks at the tele-screen. Shapes and spirits establish illusory dimension on the monitor. They are coming out at him as club & spiked bat wielding ghoulish combatants. This Mister does not play Mr. Tough Guy; he is allowing the holographic monsters to waltz about his living room. He does nothing to usurp them. They dive inside and steal his vaguely pure soul then retreat.

Same old man now empty rolls his head over his left shoulder to gaze and adore his pin up. The band members are pictured trailing in a line from in to outside a house boasting a large picturesque yard. One sits on a stool just inside a sliding glass door while another sits with his right knee propped up behind the leading left leg. The third behind is always standing forty-five degrees from about-face. The fourth lies on his back with his legs in the air. They all rotate, in turn occupying each position for beside the man inside each time on the stool. This may not seem possible, but it is not a hallucination. There is a mirror and actually each variation of the shot is imposed into this mirror each time, so it becomes smaller and trails into the upper corner. His man, Waters is seated just outside the open sliding glass door in the first largest shot; hunched somewhat forward, over his bent knee. His man because he's This Mister's first poetic inspiration; all of them are magnificent, but especially drink the water through your ears.

As the music grows in intensity; becomes more frightening, shrill; as the speed of the vibrations and the pulsing increases he is entranced with his shadow on the wall, which is visually being morphed by his confounded eyes to appear like a machination in a factory with working arms commanding chains. Swaying but rigid as if the creature were squared and cast in iron its pivoting upper torso is thoroughly distorted. Thunder rumbling cuts in an out of the speakers until all of a sudden through the speakers everything is vacuumed back like a reverse bang theory pulling the good portion of his once cherished mind far beyond him into the spaces. He looks to see where it all goes in a deep daze, like he's sick from the plague, arms beneath his legs, he's sitting on his pipe and lighter now, and has been for some time. That's why the working arms seemed so strange on the slate.

Through the mist a tribal syncopation emerges and dissonant chords are pounded into the piano like the slamming of heavy doors with brutal force; hear them slam. A paranoid man is looking around as if an intruder has entered invisibly. He takes another hit. Holding in with might the winds sent outwards; smoke is blown from his lungs spiraling and clouding the area in front of his face. His head leaning against the chair, a much delayed cough, explodes from him, and he jerks to the side. Gilmour's corkscrew tornados on the guitar swindle him beneath his seat.

Fearful, glancing about he tries to find the origin of his assailant. His sights are not keen enough however. Up above the whirlwinds carry matter and atmosphere back to the mother ship: an immense holographic cream pie hovering in the sky. Let's talk about chimerical then...them shits. More and more, the magnetic pulls from the chimerical sounds are forcing his head back. Although he breaks from the spell eventually as it dissipates each time; dying down only to recharge, he is caught up again each time as each pull is stronger. Soon there is no escaping for him, he is tripping, he is on one. His dilated pupils absorb the illusion. The organ, covering as blanket isn't harmonically arranged; spontaneity is the key that shatters locks. Wailing of pain and hate experienced in this world. The on-site manager is surely asleep by now down the walk; comfortably helpless tonight; everyone in their own vices. The candles are still burning.

Not sure of what's happening in his vicinity, he checks behind him to see if any insurgents have landed in the kitchen. He takes another hit to prepare himself for any horror. Increasingly certain that this is all a hallucination his reluctance fades though his stoned expression remains as he stares blankly at the blanket with the large and centered peace sign and random tie-dyed images crowding around. Psychotic images wave and faces' mouths chant. It's ingenious though terrifying as infamy.

He looks at the TV. It glows and snows; outlined creatures battle each other on screen. They sweat and decompose. They gossip about him, he suspects, but communicate by whispers so he cannot make out the context just follow the hushed mumbles. He is lost and out of his element so he looks at his arm hairs.

All peaks end abruptly and die out. The tribal procession grows dismal grows depressing, takes on a funerary character. Something is glowing before his eyes: the dying fire. The catacombs are crying. His coherence is failing. He stands up as the organ beckons him to the stairs. He figures this is his reckoning. He aims to leave the masses at ease? Correct. He expects them not to read this embellished memoir. In this laboratory all the vanquished desires can be cataloged. He habitually avoids exerting enough effort to broadcast as an individual. This does not mean he's a follower, he is actually a recluse. Someone is chanting to him, speaking the word from the inside as if it were spiritual council. He stops his climb on the fifth step and sits down sideways bracing the step. His right foot is planted on the fourth step. His elbow is propped on the sixth step. He feels uneasy about revival. He is just being random. He is a young adult with no plan. He knows only of his dreams concerning their desertion. He knows only to have been ridiculed enough to abandon the arts that are therapy to his soul. He may seem like an artist still, but it is all a routine. There is no divine spark. There really is a lack of creativity. There is no longer any reason to aspire as far as he's concerned. He takes the last hit from his pipe which is ass. Through his countenance he relates the emotional information that finds its way into this coulda, woulda, shoulda been minimalist exposition. If you could see his eyes, the truth would be apparent and the above testimony would not seem as mere assumptions. If you understood enough about his symbolism you would not need the narrator and would simply deduce.

He rests his head on the barrier, holding his breath. He exhales; a faint stream is propelled forward. He sparks the lighter in his left hand. Is it perfectly coincidental or an immaculate hallucination: the presence of a flower in a burnt sienna plastic pot with green leaves, and a deep purple blossomed bud on the eighth step? It does not move it does not wither. Only his vision distorts it. It stays there in perfect health and casts a shadow. It is a depressing flower nonetheless, because he dubs it as such, speaking softly, like his voice is extinguished, it is raspy.

"Who has the access?"

The flame from the lighter is not extinguished by his breath. He keeps the gas lever depressed. The blue flame sheltered by the cooler orange glow is petrified inside. It is blown by some breeze. The matter to the man is the moment: so visible and peaceful that without trying he starts crying to the soundtrack.

The organ's bass pedals rattle the speaker cone, its accompanying progressive melody blares out the tweeter.

Slumber ensues when the song ends. His head hangs down where his chin rests in his collar. He's let go of the lighter but the flower is still there. Has someone left it there? He doesn't want to see anymore. He doesn't want it to be anymore. He doesn't want to be either. Maybe there is still more there to tell. He is still yet to step into the white fire like the Dante he's read about.

Where is the deity; a shade? Will he reach the clouds in formation someday this week? The sun can rise for affectionate dandelions whose heads are blown by any indiscriminant gust.

The TV is left downstairs to blare and glare and for the snow behind the screen to gather into forms that look like teardrops and within their membrane present a magnified view of cells in mitosis to demonstrate asexual reproduction. Holographic modern children of age exit the screen and perform in the living room as if it's an amphitheatre. He wishes they'd pipe down, or skedaddle out through a warp pipe.

The marooned purple flower on the steps has vanished. He runs down the stairs as soon as the next track "see-saw" begins to stop the player so he doesn't have to endure the lighthearted tune. There he is caught up by the raucous in his living room and the imagery until he shakes it up like an etch-a-sketch. Now, all the way to the throne atop the case he goes with his wicker basket, setting it on the eighth step and continuing solo. He turns on the light and closes the door.

Sitting down and insecure on the toilet with the door closed behind him, he brings his pants down only to the edge of his knees. He sits down on the toilet for the last shit of his life and it's feeling strange to flush his system. He feels pressured to execute; pushing his penis pointing down into the pot. He sings to himself a few lines about his physic emanations flowing, from Pink Floyd's "Let there be more light", ironically the opening track to "The Saucer" LP he was just playing a track from. It goes: "Summoning his cosmic power/and glowing slightly from his toes/his psychic emanations flowed". And with that urine flows.

Rocking forth in distress to his knees, he makes the needed squeeze and the stool, is not one to sit on. He then reaches to his left side for his roll of teepee: his defense mechanism. He finds it and unrolls the spool. He sits up proper and with his left hand behind his back wipes the anus clean, scraping up from the taint. He fingers inside the sphincter which is still open, and cleans any clinging feces.

His feces being not completely solid matter looses mass as it slithers around in the bowl and rears, like a hog or some perturbed animal, its snout struggling to surface.

What is necessary is also habit, is also soothing, until excessive scratching causes rashes. He stands up and pulls up his pants looking at the edible European flatfish: a turbot, being flushed down. He watches the water twirl around in vertigo; vacuumed into the cavernous tunnel to the catacombs of this cities sewer system. He caresses the toilet seat, wishing the pilgrims a good voyage—mixing all sorts of metaphors just as his shit is a conglomeration of food stuffs.

* * 14 * *

This Mister remains in the bathroom still, looking himself in the mirror. He turns the faucet on and rinses his hands, he uses soap to sanitize then he rinses them again then finally he splashes water up on his face and rubs his palms down slowly, stretching his flesh. He eventually is through with entertaining himself and then slicks back his hair before he exits; he leads himself out the bathroom door.

He rushes downstairs to mute the volume on the television. At this time, which is the only time immediately accessible, he wishes to plunge into the cave. He wishes to pronounce the sound. He wishes to speak "Ummagumma."

He pulls out the saucer of sound from the tray and puts it back in its case. He reaches from a green sleeve containing the jewel cases to two CDs and retrieves the studio mix. The repetitious dark poster now has its chance to delight with true flavor. The candles for the shrine still grow melodiously.

He is hovering over the kitchen table writing on the back off the page he wrote the poem kept private during dinner in a sharper, smaller crayon. On this page he writes a new phrase supposed to be spoken by the almost forgotten face the caption [proverb] was smudged out above. The log reads: 'Springtime, tuck me in'.

He drinks half of what is left of the juice, and leaves along with it, the page propped open by the plastic sack of substance. Also the bread is still beside, hinting at what might be in the refrigerator.

He reaches above him for the red horn and unscrews it from the fixture. He looses it to the linoleum, and then feels for warts on his thumbs, because he's been worrying so much.

He turns off the chandeliers as the vulgar chords ring. He feels as if he were in Kashmir; everything is becoming brown. He must be making his descent. He obtains an apple & a paper towel, then his paints & brushes on the way

Guided by the light of the TV he ventures out, intrigued by the chalky piano keys. The music strikes sore ears like the droplets created by the kicking of a swimmers poised feet. He is sitting again as he was on the case. The swimmer's kicks grow jittery and the tonality more dissonant. Rick Wright is randomly pressing keys all over the place. A fat lip and chin protruding from the wall in the stairwell mouths something at him.

"Shut the fuck up!"

He takes a huge bite out of his green apple. But it is so tart; it is not good. Sock! Then stumbling down the stairs; the munched particles: chunks he's let fall out of his mouth off his tongue, smacking a big bite out.

Another procession, the integration of all foreshadowed knowledge into a self-image with regard to symbolic context to the tune of a thunderous piano and drums; he begins to paint, squeezing burnt sienna on his filler brush, waiting for the coming of the most apocryphal melodies from the keys.

He paints curved lines above him concave-down forming a shape much like a guitar pick to a rattling drum beat with dungeon contraptions and theatric wailing. The light comes from the bathroom atop the stairs. Beasts up there are tortured, whipped, and procured. Opening their mouths a little louder they shriek like swinging doors if doors could be horrified. He quits trying to peek. "If you don't want to be blurred out, you better mind your own business", he reminds himself. He begins to scrape at the wall very fast, moving his brush back and forth violently to fill in and block out the screams of the clinging lives up there. He's painting a slightly reddish-brown all over the wall. He completes the outline of what he reckons to be his alienated face. It tethers him around the axis of his psychoanalytic puss. The rattling of dungeon chains soon fades, soon the Pink Floyd are digging a new movement. He receives it's outro as a mockery of "Silent Night" on the organ with dropping bass and the entry of a babbling brook during the fade out. It is actually, "SYSYPHUS PART FOUR" by Richard Wright.

But it has not ended: suddenly there is a percussive and piping scream with a fermata over it and it reverberates loudly throughout the loft. The apocalypse is imminent while he shapes the features he wants promiscuous. Pounding and begging for mercy with his brush and green now, experimenting with the skin tone adding viridian to the mix. Internally his mind is hosting litigators debating the intentions of those commanding the hovering craft nosily operating overhead while he's trying to paint. Gleaming, vibrating, and hovering it fades out like a picture is cut out by failing transmission. He's singing this song softly with an alto vocal:

The driving force to let a mind slip away
To vanquish the feelings of happiness
In a momentary lapse
The hours seem pleasantly to coexist

When all light fades from the day and a soul lay in prayer to die
To not have the warmth of the sun make the beads on his brow
To not know the beauty of a woman
To not understand what he has left unstudied

To put an end to experience
Is the most impertinent being, being disruptive?
By terminating
Prematurely

Vagrant beasts and manlike transients are only in recess while the sampled birds chirp to he who slouches, bedazzled in "GRANCHESTER MEADOWS" with the lyrical Waters. As soon as he drifts off they return malicious as ever—crazy-making. They emit syncopated howls and other odious noises from the banister. Even from the rafters predators lurk. Then Roger returns, howling and carrying on like a hyena in a studio booth in the background; no longer singing poetically. He's vaguely speaking English. During his acoustic program minutes ago it was like he'd merely come out for a spell from a perverted ride through Splash Mountain. Now while the soprano's wail he feels as if he's on a log dropping down a chasm.

In the new program Roger returns to slap him with some crazy stuttered dialect he can almost make out. He tries and again he's there with his hand rested near the apple core at his side while Roger growls then roars. And talks about being dead as something the wind cried back at; and someone is thankful to it or him, someone utters 'thank you' just after Roger finishes. He swears to have heard something swatting the animals against a solid panel even though it is rumored they are only gathered and grooving with a pict (whatever that is). Animals are being bludgeoned upstairs; mark This Mister's words with a yellow highlighter.

His restless, weakening body, shield of near silence; he must pass out in the loft, on the platform. Some rustling winds spirals with an increasing sonic intensity toward sending him pawing up the stairs by the apple pi painting: a large painting of a green apple with a bite taken out of it. One of a series of paintings in which he trailed pi out, copying it from his calculus book onto panel after panel. This was number three, the numbers where in yellow on the brown white chunk taken out through the skin. He's into the bathroom once again.

* * 15 * *

He stands there in the bathroom, rubbing his finger on dry glass creating: 'rhrrhn-rhrrprhnn' with the friction. He feels his hands and turns his hair, twisting it all back around his head and rotates it counter-clockwise into a bun while David Gilmour strums his guitar and all these synthesized sounds screech by or seem to be touching down, and taking off. He keeps wrapping his hair up until it is tightly wound. He then pushes flat all his hair and dreadlocks lying down tips forward, except for the back one, the flattest club which still trunks out. He hears some noise like footsteps and turns around to leave the bathroom. He stops and looks through his banisters, descending into a dry bed waiting at the bottom of the staircase; he pokes his head between the bars. The lights upstairs, none of them are on. The only light is coming from the cracked bathroom door, unable to contain all the light inside it. There are new frightening chords of a marching tribal brigade. He is lost in Africa on a plateau. His eyes try to focus on a flashing clocking between two mattresses. He ponders on the odd amount of hours he's required to develop his ultimatum.

He is prepared to forsake all, to revoke his life, and be belittled no longer, to feel no longer disrespected, and mocked behind his back. He hates to lie and outsource pain.

His pain, of the last five years—he will vanish from his flesh. This Mister will not have to take over the family business. It's a death job; a plague. It doesn't matter how hard his father worked for it to sustain his family. He shouldn't have left it in such a fragile state.

How compassionate right? We will all be young once.

With the right kind of determination, he may be absolved. That is what through pondering he rationalizes. Confirmation acknowledges his suspicions sometimes but only after extensive simulated periods focused on assimilating into a vexed state, as he is in now. Perplexity of the solo missions and the long passed group excursions is astounding.

He follows the speaker's chants up the shafts into the ceiling, looking for the rodents gnawing at the structure; like termites, like vermin, like disease. Someone is always crying; is it he inside? It can't be Id. All night long Id has thrived. Is it his ego, bruised?

"Fuck it."

That's conscientious enough...right?

Can his feelings clearly be projected since his mind is too saturated by death? He treads back up onto the sleeping platform and leans back on his elbows on his mattress to stare at the oblong white wall. Bright flashing light terrorizes. It is then he realizes on his way, he switched on a strobe light. It is pulsing rapidly. Echoing baboons musically repeat the phrase Wheeeeeeeeeeeeeeee each time they finish a verse, they're sliding down a tree. He turns his back innocently gathering the input; scrambling to imprint his depression on the painting in the stairwell.

Outside, down somewhere over the edge of the balcony, in almost total darkness, the screams find a frequency to emit but it is not so clear and the wails waver. When he turns away the wooden teeth from broken skateboards begin laughing at him. Recalling his flailing and tangled body, contorting itself into a bruising or other clumsily imposed predicament; he's all but given up skateboarding, for the time being; all but given up on a fulfilling adolescent experience all together.

"My would-be friends just don't understand. I never clamored at them like that"

Like what.

"At all! Shut…the fuck…up!!!".

He stands near the banister, and empties his pockets of everything except his pastels which ends up being some scraps of paper, possibly a napkin and some coin.

He treads into the stairwell again shaking his head and snarling. He seems on the verge of delivering a devilish verbal philippic. He rights with white pastel [The [Alien [Inside [Me] on the forehead of his alien face. Then quickly as in a spasm he grabs the fine brush and in ebony outlines the features shaped earlier, like the eyes, and nostrils. Then he wipes the brush and for the first time acquires a tiny bit of French ultramarine to further blue his already blue-green lips. This alien certainly is blessed with melanin. This psychedelic depiction of some mystic he presumes, for the way he regards him is in awe and disbelief. It could be the psychedelics with his eyes. He's still shaking his head in shock somewhat.

He wipes the fine brush one last time, obtains some antique white and applies a small ring in the eye; very thin for the pupils of this messenger are dilated as well. There is no apparent iris. Then he reacquires a new previously neglected medium brush for some more lettering to accompany his largest painting yet. This Mister was in fact painting spastically for the better part of a forty minute program which is approaching, second by second, its final throes. The painting is nearly the size of two posters. He squeezes the oil onto the brush over the basket and them proceeds to letter: [We[Need[Real[Light]

He has always had the answers in possession to the questions he never needed to ask. It's plum fun to assume the rhetorical air as long as one doesn't get stuffy like British intellectuals or Ivy League alumni. It is easier to believe and lie to your concerned self that your faith hasn't dissipated, that the high is still there. It is foolish to trust your deceitful hopes. You know they'll leave you four million miles away from the root of what you struggle against. He means to speak out loud but he just whispers these things in confidence to the narrator who is betraying him this very instant. Are these sounds just bringing the darkness out of him? Is there a problem with that...anywhere?

Anyways, this suicide inside may not be an answer in the slightest; it may just be a novella.

He paints a green tower from the top down to the forehead. He roots the rook to the alien head. He paints a flag pole then gets his white paint tube; he attempts to indicate his surrender but the green on his brush that he did not wipe clean leaves a muddy trace over the area he wished his banner to be displayed. He is afraid the no one will recognize his plea for amnesty. He is without love. He is depressed. He is alone. He joined the wrong crowd that has dissipated now and he is through with the work, with his art and most of all he is sick from the disrespect he perceives. This Mister sounds like one of his spoiled enfants. He must have consumed too many.

Look beyond you, can you even? What happens if you are too far in? Where there is no shining light? What if your soul does no longer glow? If you have drowned in the abyss, if you are one with noir, if your depression has long since stated it's maturity, what can you do but not go out, but not face tomorrow? Your cries do not rise to your own lips often. There isn't a partner to spare some time, someone to pay mind, and turn the nice boy away from the dark side. There is no tissue for the tears that shed from the eyes that can never hide the hurt inside.

He makes his way down the stairs. Gilmour's composition "THE NARROW WAY" comes to a close. Gilmour has sung to him as he treaded north through dark corridors. Gilmour asks him if he wants to stay a little bit, if he wishes to rest his aching limbs. Gilmour is right he can't delay, "he hears the night birds calling/and no he can't catch exactly what they say/ because of the growing roar exactly. Gilmour's lyrics are in this narration to suit the prose. Now if it's all just the same, and surely, he to has seen hope before—until it dissolved. So David if it's all the same and since he doesn't want to stay, if it's all just the same and since the program inevitably progresses, if it's all just the same and since you approve, if it's all just the same and since This Mister does not wake up to love which is the life force each morning, if it's all just the same he is now to enter in time in to "THE GRAND VIZIERS GARDEN PARTY". There was so much darkness in the last installment: some terrible march underway in the corridor. This Mister virtually shuffles past the transitioning spirits chattering and throwing their heads back in laughter. Such spite does he possess. Does This Mister repress? You bet.

He's on the last step until he steps onto the ground floor. He mopes over to the car bucket seats. He sits down on the one nearer to the sliding glass door. He looks outside totally exhausted and scared out of death. The flute is somewhat comforting until it is interrupted by Nick Mason's drum roll transitioning with a cymbal crash into his psychedelic, echoing toms.

Maybe it isn't worth it, but whatever happens, it is too late to bargain. The toxicity in this palace must be increasing by the minute.

Why not just turn it off? To prove a point. Perhaps This Mister should have mentioned, his mother's side of the family hails from Germany. Thus he is both stubborn & passionate, just as he is both a Cancer & a Leo. It's the pits really to be born on the cusp in July.

In haste he gets up and walks over by the corner of his desk where the cords that control the blinds file through the small space. First he grabs the straight rope cord and pulls it sending the blinds, moving down the line, almost to the rhythm of the echoing drums played by Mason himself. He tilts the bike away from the sliding glass window so that the blinds don't get caught up. He next pulls the beaded cord that files the blinds about face. It is early morning. It is almost dawn he supposes, though he doesn't know how the night has passed. Maybe he's tripping and it's barely three a.m. At any rate the *garden party's entertainment* is of the most vacuous nature. Perfect for him to paint along to which is what he is inclined to immediately pursue.

He ventures upstairs in the dark. Upon his climb he attains his paints and sits before the oblong white wall and the strobe light. In his darkest brown; the burnt umber he scrapes the tube against the wall in a line that is more like a mountain ridge than a roadway.

He paints back into the distance from his line with his thickest brush the threshing floor, the surface: ground. It looks like cratered land like he's painting the desolate landscape of some satellite. He adds some of the yellow ochre to his brush over the umber and for no one he writes [landscapes]. Then he decides the word needs a prefix to fill in the space so he chooses the word [void]. Then with the ebony tube This Mister scratches eleven hash marks side by side, but spaced enough to span across the whole of his horizontal plane. With the medium brush he brushes down the rather thick hash marks the glob of oil down, creating eleven rather long, practically spear length but very crooked marks. This is to represent the sky or atmosphere presumably or a hail of awkward javelins showering down, not yet to the ground. With all the excess black on his brush he quickly outlines the portrait of a human body, head to toe—silhouetting. It lay atop the barren landscape. There is enough vacuous space within its boundaries to be a vessel for a phrase.

Quickly finishing now fortunately he has his towel to wipe the medium brush now before he applies what is to be the final touch. He is already looking back at the painting like he's satisfied with its minimalist composition. He applies vermillion and a dab of black onto the same medium brush and begins to letter another code. Within the cranium he marks [i]. Where the heart should be beating is the language symbol [think]. In his diaphragm he letters [i'm]. In his pelvis [dying], at his knees: [right], and finally at his feet the word [now] is lettered. Without a martyr there is no veneration and he could have been anybody. This was all his choice, possibly not his plan though. The slogan reads [I[thiNk[i'm[DyINg[Right[nOW].

Mason solos on the tympanis to finish off. This Mister sits huddled up wrapping his arms around his knees. He is by now a hollowed shell; barely a legal adult. The landscape is bare yet pleasant. It is time to ride the night, to be charged the ultimate price, to end this life.

"Buy the ticket, take the ride *right?"*

When all the flesh & substance that is fit to print is consigned to a vessel, naught but the skeletal remains. This is the case. This Mister must be afraid of change. Whistles approach from the background over Mason's battering.

Bon voyage!

His disappointed crowd will be taxed for his actions. But his exit, this departure will excuse his absence from any future luncheons. He falls back onto his futon mattress on the floor. He lay back amongst his finished paintings, his guitar, a telescope, a bagged snowboard, a hoard of records with one tower of speakers by his head. He rests his head on a naked pillow which is stacked atop another pillow beneath it: a pillow he made in fifth grade that has his name and some trifle symbols now part of his antiquated childhood. He pulls his khakis off, and puts on a pair of sweat pajamas that were his fathers and are all stained with paint from projects past.

He is at home now, waiting in a realm. He pulls his brown blanket over him: the one he used to share with his wilted specter of a woman. He kept all the trinkets hoping she'd be resurrected but alas—preoccupation.

On his left side is a stack of mostly inoperable machinery. Half of it is silver, the other half black: two different models of home stereo equipment. The only thing that does work is the record player which is set atop of the banister because it is so sensitive to any movement on the ground, like say walking. One of the receivers can be powered on to operate therefore everything exists still though it is mostly outdated garbage. The record player emits a sonic signal out of the higher set of speakers stacked in tower fashion in the corners against the banister. They face out towards the sloping ceiling and giving the whole area good sound coverage. The architecture of the compartment provides for great acoustics. There is usually a record loaded played but stopped midway through.

This theory is corroborated by the sleeve leaning against the front posting the milestones that Elton John erected with many classic tunes. He powers on the receiver. Instantly there is sound. It drags for a second but Elton distinctly belts out "are free to fly, high away, bye-bye". It is not likely one will save his life tonight. He'll let this die out then follow suit; slightly smarter than the man saved from his marriage to Sugar Bear; crying for help at four o'clock in the morning. The music keeps playing slowly getting out of the way for the next song. This Mister waits for the figurative truck to take him home.

Any final thoughts?

"It's not a job; it's a duty & I can dig that."

What about the last chapter? Peep the narrator backpedaling reactively.

"I'll just pretend this moment of clarity didn't occur and repent tomorrow."

Really, how long have you been considering this?
"The whole time"
Very well, repent tomorrow…if you survive this night Mister.
"I'm going to bed."

* * Prelude to an End * *

When it is easier to happily walk into death than to stay awake through the trip and watch the sunrise. Like the first when all was so new and you stayed awake to draw pictures in a lawn chair in your driveway. Art measures humanity, material neglected. This scheme has ventured into the depths, be assured: it is not intelligent gentlemen. These are real and confusing matters, you are a real and confusing person. That you realized it is impossible to make art happen, impresses no one. So, it's an attitude, so your mind effortlessly creates at its disposal. So you've learned how to recognize things other than the marvelous paintings, other than the visionary writers, and all glorious cinematographers who master their art form. You are bedazzled by the feminine quality of rolling foothills. You are bedazzled by the texture of vomit. You are confounded by, yet endeared to the way two indifferent humans interact. All is special and deserves regard but to life there's only more. All you who seek to live beyond this evening better have learned to observe and listen in your adolescence. For in adulthood you must be dedicated to enhancing your social prowess, and becoming absolutely comfortable with your character and position in public.

It's true you've learned to decipher symbols, to discern tone, to interpret nature, and to...well you can't say you very well empathize—seeing as you are solely preoccupied. Other than that—you learned to gauge with six senses. You've tried to extract a feeling form everything. However, you've mulled over your woes and where not able to let the easy groove work its way into your flow. You've pleaded for the removal of objects from your existence, but could not rid them for yourself. You were afflicted and consequently in your bitterness were offensive to fend off. There was no help, no confidence. You've so boldly declared disdain for life itself, all oppressive forces, and ridiculing social normatives you overtly sensitive prickly pear.

You've felt humiliated, disrespected, and dehumanized. You've donned filters to color, distort, and debase every exchange. You've formed habits of compulsive behavior. You are undermined and unsuccessful, say you. You've absolved nearly all concern for your health. You are excluded because you did not allot energy to vie for inclusion. You've retracted, now you desire to retire—or do you howl for release; to be urged on, invited in, or truly intrigued?

You are torn or in denial; confounded by an acquired indecisiveness. You think possibly you've narrowed it down, but can't be sure, and if so –have no clue as to—HOW?

You've endured the disintegration helplessly; never considering your actions deliberate, or these events anything but inevitable. You do not recognize how you have flushed yourself away as an accumulated heap of festering waste. Now you are flustered; courting damnation. Now you are eager to admit: you are weak, a nonconfrontationalist; a pleading separatist who can't bear to be referred to as a person, much less address himself in the first person.

I always sound like I'm accusing someone of some violation. It's repulsive of me. I know I aspire to be a Medicine Man but in reality I am naught but a Misery Maker.

I feel so guilty please…pardon me for never allowing a proper introduction myself. Pardon me for counting myself out, and for convincing myself it's too late to change. I know, I just want to kill my mom and have it my way.

None comprehend the anguish I care less to showcase. I am evil and everyone resents me. This makes me a selfish and self-righteous alien ostracized, and this loft is not even a sanctuary. I am inextricably plagued by my defeatist thoughts. Better yet, or most of all: I'm at my best, when I feel the worst and I become as an anti-climactic messiah where I don't have to prove anything to anybody but…I probably can be entertaining. Unfortunately now I need to never have been, as sleepy as I am presently. So without further adieu—

I'm dying…from thinking…

I'm always hearing that film exec. from Woody Allen's Stardust Memories say, **"I've seen it all before, they document their own private suffering and pawn it off as art."**

What a cunt.

* * Epilogue * *

The spirit of the petrified youth is thrown upon the oblong wall. A holographic image huddled inside a corner of a grand seized bunker spreading pages of illustration as fortification. He's trying to project some semblance of insanity wearing a sinister smirk over where his motorized mouth should run off. He rocks back and forth looking tired but wired and wide open, gazing dispassionately over his arc of artwork.

In a consternated state, assuming the grimace appropriate, even necessary if he's in the process of...say: reviewing and revising an oral history currently under scrutiny or perhaps presently being invented and committed to memory like some sacred text, only the deluded believe it to be...truly lonely......he is......the way he is for some reason or another.

The image dissipates as his sense of hearing degenerates until all is a haze clinging to the surface before the wrapped segmented insect gestating and awaiting transmutation. The sequence is a projection in the third eye of This Mister (the new age Kafkaesque scarab). He can barely hear the record playing.

The young man lay wrapped, as if already embalmed like a sarcophagus, blanket pulled over, around and tucked under his entire body, head included. Free falling to the earth is anything but exhilarating; actually rather embarrassing and uneventful.

Each drawn breath is incrementally fainter. Static settles around the body. Time used to take forever and catalogue it. Now there is reason to employ.

Wrapped in what more appropriately deserves to be considered a cocoon, the young man is hella frozen. Here in the vicinity of this passage the indecisive unwitting attributes of Almin Ailen are quintessentially showcased. Almin Ailen is to the mixing of metaphors, a bit deranged and crazy himself. If he was comfortable enough to freestyle some final words, perhaps he'd speak, just to expel some extra breath. But he checks powerlessly. He does however register some satisfactory gain in esteem, rationalizing psychically*: it's better, more beautiful I didn't just shoot heroin into both arms and with the blast of a shotgun jerk still.*

Somewhere near the bridge of, "Don't let the Sun Go Down on me" some person pries open the sliding glass door and parts the blinds quietly, as if intending to be courteous. Possibly a lover, possibly a thief crosses the den onto the linoleum. He stoops over the offering, examining the sack weight on the open book of pocket poems. He keeps the page marked while he's appraising the stress buds then when he's returned the bag, he snaps off a morsel of pita bread to test how fresh/stale it is with his free hand. It does snap. Finally he samples the imitation boysenberry juice. No it's definitely not brandy and blood, a.k.a. Sangria.

So far it's just a little eerie.

The Stinker a.k.a. The lover/thief, treads deeper into the dead-end corridor, creeping right by the oven, noticing nothing out of the ordinary. He opens the refrigerator and within 6 seconds all the conditioned air escapes as the door is held open and the stinker indulges in the sight of all the uncovered dishes. He cocks his head to the side like a B-boy. Then looks down and notices the goop beneath his shoes. He notices the nomenclature on the rind.

"Almin used to call me Arnie affectionately; what's happening?" The stinker whispers.

The door's never locked. It's as quiet as a strangled cock. Almin is a deep breather.

Just a little more eerie.

He lifts his chin and after staring at it for a series of seconds his brain finally realizes what is not literally right under his nose. This development is too real to astonish him. The oven is on and propped open by Almin's fave-wooden-spoon, the one his mom used to whack him with when he'd behaved rotten. Almin used to reminisce about that spoon, but not as much as about how he loved to put it to good use in those days, and in this present as well. Rather than shriek the lover/thief merely backs up a tad so he can brace adequately.

This cannot be.

He's pushed the refrigerator door to the end of the corridor forcing a hefty chunk of wood leaning to a vertical position upon it is the Stinker's own self-trait as the lover/thief that about a year ago he, himself, Lessur, painted when he used to, before he used to, no *when?* He used to reside here. It's all very astonishing and sudden, his memory is flashing, or lapsing, but this is not the right time to relax…so?

He turns around and steps out of the way to push the refrigerator door closed (was that at all loud?) when he's caught gazing in exasperation at the scene. Atop the broken board in yellow is painted the words *lover/thief* with a thinned acrylic. Silhouetted in a blustery storm is a nervous burlap-wrapped man looking over his shoulder with two stone-cut eyes and a long breaking frown.

The Stinker turns back around noticing how aware he is now at the moment. After an instant of horror, he yanks forth the spoon from the oven as if he were the chosen, one also known as: Arnie. He drops the spoon then and really, with new eyes, scans the scene: *holy oils!* Reliefs cover the walls.

This intruder is a compatriot of Almin Ailen's, the petrified male an indecent docent, a self-absorbed, multi-faceted being less than charming enough to impress anybody, and stealing all 99.9% of the limelight.

This compatriot mobbed over from the Amtrak upon conclusion of a very personal sojourn. Lessur Martain, former roommate, best-good friend may well rise as a savoir by virtue of an impeccably orchestrated arrival. Lessur rode from Reno, where he'd spent days visiting with his mother. It was the last monumental summit in a desperately necessary leave of absence from everything Almin Ailen. Lessur hopped on an earlier train than the one he originally planned would drop him into town early the next afternoon in the middle of the night, during the first haunted of this day he began his trek across Fresno, from downtown and into Clovis, absently homebound. What he has here, horribly contrived…is an obvious plea for bargain.

In a very funny way, *I beg your pardon.*

Lessur Martain is the cult Chaplin of BMP (the Boyish Mannequin Parade) He also founded the society of The Walking Dead TWD, in fact, prior to the inception of the BMP. It is safe to say, *Lessur tires easily,* with identities. Almin Ailen is the one ugly enough with ambition to compose charters without the collective input of members. He's never believed they recognized him whole-heartedly. Almin Ailen perceives himself as the perennial outsider privately. Not good enough for the TWD. He spawned TWdartain *as it seems to persist these days,* to retaliate in the first place. They were partners in art, Lessur before Almin, fairly new artists, rare brash men with individual prerogatives.

Alas all Almin considered compatriots, especially Lessur apparently became irrevocably disenchanted by Almin Ailen and the want of attention, driving Almin in his loneliness to declare ultimatum status as if to threaten his fellows. The designs Almin had on Lessur's girl are unsettling. He was saddened to realize each individual had derived visions of the end-design, cherished. Pity the groups that's not thinking in harmony, but you can't.

Perhaps that's all aside now or...under the bridge, after this long, undefined while; with Lessur's return, it probably would be inept to offer him water.

Few know this. It was a latent epiphany that terribly discombobulated Almin Ailen.

Did I wish for god to have you daddy
because of my little fantasies of being
ostracized from the family by your passionate face and now I live this hell for
siding with mommy who was cool to a young boy, but now I am a belonging
I knew you never excluded me from celebrations w/ family father, but
you could be terrifying.

Life is abuse and
we are living.

Almin Ailen is the result, hanging on, snagged some might say by a thread as the wreck in disguise, as the fool figuratively stoking fire inside who parted that blinding ultraviolet whiteness he appeared through the midst of, wheeling in his antiquated bike with a backpack and bag(s) of groceries. Now, treacherously, in disbelief, Lessur scales each step individually, silently pressing carpet with the balls of his feet; careful not to disturb the worst fears and agitate them into actuality.

Ironically playing? It's the tune "Sorry seems to be the Hardest Word."

The best-good friend a man can have is upstairs finding the gesture of a static human not exactly romantic.

"**Good Morning Robin Williams**" he says.
But nothing.

Wake, wake man, I call you because you can not see the god who placed the light. You lay within your loft upon a level where it is dark. Wake-wake, young man who scurries away trying to carry all his papers; this grand seized bunker is not your home. Wake-wake man—after you learn to breathe. Wake, wake you will real soon for your terrible bony head. Come on! Pacific Gas & Electric, not gas from the electric ocean dummy there's nothing worse than being a pseudo-alchemist. There're no toxins in the atmosphere you're frying. It's deranging put simply. Friends later. Where's the grease-fire? wake-Wake! Man, are you more impassioned or liar? Or are you right?

Lessur Martain never really paid attention to the mechanics of the stovetop and oven. He mostly ate little Debbie cakes and turkey jerky sticks. So he suddenly reserves his wrath.

Lessur Martain comes around to pity his former roommate. He knows a worn man who's been through a share of everything. He knows a man who doesn't know how to surrender. Lessur never thought he'd see the day when Almin submitted. It's a sad moment.

Lessur tugs on the blanket; it is tucked all around his body. His grill is gonna be sweaty when he wakes. Lessur leaves him to get it. Almin is safe from the disturbing rays of daylight, but only by the grace of architects and engineers. It's convenient which is, nothing to marvel at.

The truth Almin will wipe from his brow this evening, some sixteen hours from now, outside of his cocoon, or from his sarcophagus—rid of his umber bedding, which drapes over exactly like the brown comforter which shouldn't rise over the torso so extremely for any sleeping being in America.

Can Almin Ailen become a new flying creature, taking off into the visions of his mind to recover from a near fatal dive with an expedience, none other than miraculous for only Lessur, if he's even present, to see?

Unconcerned with what next is to ensue, Lessur Martain ventures downstairs to viddy the number done on the dwelling and to grub on the dish so generously prepared. *'Who's the prince'* Lessur's thinking, *'this knig hasn't even read Machiavelli'.* That's the contention spawned cerebrally from the true Jew of Kings.

Lessur however particularly is intrigued by *the alien inside of me*: turquoise green and brown pic-headed creature, which had made him the most apprehensive in the moment, scaling the set. Now to him it looks like great art, worth at least a shrug.

He steps back through the kitchen and paces absently. After opting to smoke some of what looks like a ½ of Gadbury's stress relief he steps back into the den to reads Almin's beliefs just above a whisper.

Almin necessarily didn't share much of his private poetry with his fellow so this occasion is special and awkward.

"denatured
subsequently
depressing flower
feeling inadequate

hammering self
with overwhelming explanations
of salvation

fuck! To calm down
or talk—
relating "

that's all

this is all I want to do

but there'll be a day when I will no longer entertain this fantasy

Truman Capote
is in another room
and had a dynamic integrity
that surpassed others
he might as well be
man of the century

SO YOU MAY HOLD THE SUN IN YOUR HANDS

i

The coast was dark and we were dreary. We were looking for the man with the bag because what would he pull? We had only feet and were well into the dunes. Miles from the shore though we could still see its line. Newly risen moon was smiling. Taunting other was to roast us come morning.

We knew not the definite nature of what we sought. We called him man but he was more likely entity. Seemingly we were internally debating our posthumous situation—wading through silences as shades. We were not discussing our differing opinions. I couldn't hear even the insect symphonies, as of yet no quarreling entities, only the sand, shifting.

ii

When there is nothing else to do, nothing to quench any imaginable need, we will not need to stop. We will walk, dead. We had been since before dusk. Since just after our car sputtered to a halt. Hours elapsed. We were slow to mobilize. We knew not what distance we would travel.

We trekked the day away unawares. We did not regard. We could not know anything as exactly as we were fatigued by solar rays. We struggled to discover how we could somehow shed the solar cloak. I realized I don't know how at all to be a man. I've noticed we are nothing more than the attention we pay.

At long last the light dissipated and now the moon is rising ahead, in our direct line of sight. Brilliance now stokes the shimmering sector of the satellite gloriously facing earthlings in this region. The remaining portion of the hemisphere is horridly cold; darkened and a blur in the atmospheric canopy enveloping.

I've toiled the depth of the fathomed universe. Always being real doesn't render well being; ambiguous as the heavens were conceived. I could ultimately be one fleeting matey streaming. I may never alert any to praxis; may remain a separatist—however, our gathered formation could be reasoned.

The purpose afforded this flight is exodus. This very journey acts on measures deliberated to prevent future famishes from announcing hurt. We cannot build here.

The gradual disintegration of coherence will have us marooned in these expansive dunes. It could be worse. Looking abroad I note: our epidermal suits, regardless of their melanin content, seem pale in comparison to the fluorescent lunar mass orbiting light years away.

I am prone to dictating. Here I begin rambling, as if it is being recorded in the vast memory banks of the atmosphere:

"...Desert...beach is lost...dunes...out of reach ruins...only looking for something to expound on...only finding trouble...A pretense...anxious feelings...loss of coloration...more than a notion..."

iii

Scanning the unfamiliar company of the others representing a part of us three sharing glances. The historical collection of particulars regarding these fellows soars free beyond my mental grasp, through my ears, guided by tandem furies. My silenced and amnesic self grows forlorn by the instant. It continues to mark time by the step however, trudging on to the timely tune of scuffing.

I fret presently over inability to synthesize relevance of events, which invite mysterious plight devices to incite fright. I wake from derelict observations and make notes privately.

Intuitively our company derives energy to propel through situational impasse. The gelatin consistency of atmosphere is cited as a detrimental force hindering progress.

Just why is my accessibility dissolving? I have to focus on concentrating, it is not coming naturally. Now wait, what is this approaching pulse? Is it my memory about to come back to me? No, not completely but I recognize these fellows; know they are my company. I wonder on the thoughts occupying their cranial cavities. Do not know unless they tell me.

Feeling kind until profanely blaming wise others for my misery. Are we becoming inclined to immortality? Nothing anymore retains its normality. Troublesome that a gradually occurring shift has dropped abundant loads of fear on us suddenly. I was having a relatively placid walk, lost and feeling until being jarred by a sudden turbulence and annoyed by a noisome and reciprocating sonic transmission. Now, dynamic visual patterns spill all over the desert before me. I began speaking in tongues, chanting through an involved recitation of many synchronized and intonated utterances. If it was to incite the aid of an audible response, I'm not sure. I have been struggling to absorb, trying to dissect, hoping to reestablish the prominence in where I am now.

iv

The moon moves continually although sometimes it is hard to chart its progress alone with the eye. Occasionally I would find myself sleeping in my walk, though not tripping over in reflection. The anticipation of infection keeps me on my feet.

No one slowed our collective pace but we were moving rather like a curmudgeon doth travel. An occasionally cantankerous sloth dragging their daily chains of vice and malice; we are bound by our parameters. We are attached to anchors. When we escape the city limits our habits/valor do/ does not necessarily advance/increase.

I cannot believe no one has fainted out right, or passed, although I cannot really be sure any of us are awake and really moving. We could very well be fixed.

I was warily carrying the suspicion we were being steamed by some demon, or otherwise led forth unfavorably by spiritual mercenaries. They both operate in familiar ethers; one must take pains to distinguish.

v

Noxious reactions to this weighted scale, seemingly destined to remain in a state of unbalance. Such vegetation in the visuals inhibits me from perceiving the evolutionary nature surrounding. All other sound is drowned out by these incessant dialogues, dammed to house such inner monologues. I am dammed to entertain such rhetoricians and be engulfed in a continuous state of litigation. They figure I am impressionable and easy enough to convince. They should know I am very suspicious. Settling apprehension gets the feel of things; should have anticipated the anxiety, the doubt. It raises its share of hairs including all the small peachy fuzz invisible to the eye.

It will be like this for several more hours. It has already been how many? We left the shore in the afternoon, was losing it's sight by sunset, and now on our sight, who could comment rationally? As far as eyes can reason there is no sign in the landscape of any reachable destination. I turned to my mates for something; they were half-cocked eyes and wayward grins.

"...Placid creatures...hardly struggle...but they must. keep...moving...They are dead...but they...with me...are lurking..."

One more time I halt the spin, my lids; the shutters are pressured open. "Hey are you guys feeling floored?" I couldn't trust my ears to relay if they answered. "I guess I'll press on then."

How do we become so delirious—lack of vengeance? Have only to measure time by the hour, as I've recalled it. Between trance and reason I subscribe chaotically, question incessantly, pondering. How well last night had I rested? Had it been late-wandering for the last few? Were we supposed to be on the coast, camping? Today we'd been long driving. It could be this oxygen or lead poisoning no! Can it be just one thing rendering me defenseless? Why am I ever restless?

Is the cool moon draining? It's so chalky yet it glows, has a hue, a subtle translucence. Can't it quicken its pace? Won't it help feed juice to time, so that it actively passes by? But to disturb the comfortably numb—well some are on the other side, in the sun tailoring by and by and now my eyes are wider open. My head is bleeding. I check the back of my skull. Fixing my hair it's full of sand.

"I fell over."

"You were staring straight through the moon"

"I could have a head-wound."

"That is no head-wound." my friend answered back again.

My two friends, awkwardly placed, like plotted points ahead of me. Come to stand with feet. "That was pretty lively."

"Let's walk." they say.

We continue to trudge, space available to hold grudges but me, I am aided with a pair of crutches. These boys are nice, peoples reassuring that brace against the night.

vi

Progress comes in subtle shades. I'm noticing our skin is no longer as pale. The night feels like it's returning to a state of calibration. The presence of gravity is no longer as demanding. The slow wind fixing shivers must have gotten lost in the distant dunes. They'll be much warmer fevers now, thought I wouldn't put it beyond the atmosphere to revert to a low and still extremely dense arrangement of molecules suffocating to the chest cavity.

Were we supposed to inherently know in which direction to go?

I can keep getting at these variations; all pulled out of vacuous space, but never tie them down to anything concrete.

Disturbed at how distorted my private logic has become. So what, am broke and thing fine time for a crusade?

vii

Lost on the path to my memories—no access, not certain if I participated or was led on…leading? It seems like I am leading self and they are here too asserting however sensibly.

There was a car. We may have broken down and then just wandered off without thought. We may have just run out of road. Relativity of the symbol remains elusive though automobiles are prevalent in all my nightmares; layers upon layers of consciousness to be penetrated.

Thinking about our active pace, I stand to be corrected: we are still walking. I've been beguiled by my heartbeat, faint and spaced. I can feel my body shutdown between each beat. Either I'm dying or I'm living every moment to the fullest.

"...Got to get past this...got to...make it to morning..."

Wincing I look back for my friends. "We are still with you," they instinctively speak.

They were keeping pace just behind me, but why? Why such gallantry? Was it?

Were they flanking me to be safe migrating? In case I was to betray my own self silently. At this point it would be an unintentional occurrence, though...I shouldn't die here. Death is not progressive, at least not at this point: so much remains flawed. I'm unsure of the fruits of my search, what they could be, or if they are of worth so I won't bother death to stir in me. Realizing I've yet to mature along this trek, and theoretically, a mortal could survive for days on nearly nothing as long as they keep their head, and remained in their flesh.

"...Were we...or aren't we...holographic...? Am I falling... for...Is this Earth...?"

I stumble pondering upon the thought: maybe my friends could be coping worse than I. Examining them I realize I lack the omnipotence for convictions. Still I fear they could be having the same struggles as me or far more dangerous and volatile could their maelstrom be screaming on them. Yet in all actuality they could be still feeling the placid comfort of night. I may only be so affected.

My thoughts seemingly are either or. Seemingly all I have to do is choose a side. Yet there is no guessing with these choice matters. Seemingly the opaqueness of the mind clod dissipates, although I can't say it's completely evaporated. I don't feel purified on account of this newfound clarity: the either or disparity clause. It's potentially fallacious. Better go back and reevaluate my statements.

All I believe is nothing, save mathematics can produce anything resembling certainty, or model anything into perspective. I see that the moon has almost risen to the zenith. The nighttime for us for sure is passing. My observation has ground in mathematic calculation.

viii

I feel roused. I feel begotten from the night with only this one purpose: to find the man with the bag, so that we may hold the sun in our hands. I'm starting to realize this purpose may prove to be futile. Time is especially beginning to drag. Let us find your post manned, if you be material, show us a sign, your pretty, embroidered flag man.

In frustration I burst out, dictating:

"...For what...does time gratify...?"

Realizing in the term of an instant: commitment to this incident whether by choice, necessity, or by force. Out here, drifting with each elapsing moment; our histories are forgotten; being circumstantial one shouldn't fret though they would lend to our condition and explain our predispositions. Our direction is transient, and destination intangible. The odds lie with the course and destiny decides.

"Hey guys are we still traveling in the right, or are we in the way? Friends does anything appear familiar in that we would no we're going in circles, inadvertently out to sea, further into something deep, or completely, out of our heads? Isn't it so painful to distinguish?"

Experiencing already the apprehension of the nearing dawn, and the absolute delirium it brings. Sensing reluctance still we must press on, so to actively further our travels. Probably we will be cut short and perish, maybe without even leaving a print.

My thoughts can be piously pessimistic, sometimes simply pathetic. I try to control. Being in this place though is especially uncomfortable. There is nothing to protect you. I can't say it's any different from the city, where you can't even see the sky. These are hardly stars in the reaches and that lunar orb, a green shifting light—luminescent, a globe probing deeper. Purging my psyche is a featureless satellite. Each passage like each hour passes.

ix

"...Gas drifting...mist lifting fear...Queer images...molten mirages...malicious and morphing...running to them...in starvation...watching them...in dissipation...Jubilation...better find me...before I lose...every adjective...in my arsenal..."

Finally as if the story was getting weary, a glow shone from the horizon and although the sun is not yet visible I'm sure it's coming or we are lost chasing this mirage in a most unearthly abyss. But I am sure; am capable of being that way.

x

The trail trivial and trying wafted in gratefully the illuminating light. Turning around, I expected to share the glory of this sacrosanct scene however my company...was gone!

xi

Had they disappeared, had they ever been? How autistic is the way I question what's partial and relatable, shouldn't I know better? This can be nothing less than the worst, most beguiling dream this season.

What carried me away from this premonition? Honestly, can I trust that premonition, just by what happened now? What's coincidence, does it fit in? This is a very doubtful case.

They might have dropped signals about heading off on their own. There may have been an error in my receiving messages sent. Right now I am not standing well with attention. Am I simply not looking hard enough?

Searching my peripheral I see nothing. I swear there is no one. Nothing but the landscape is what I'm telling. Surreal and now glowing with relative shine, eight minutes behind. At this point with regards to my attitude I could no longer claim benign. I went daft, way past pleasant, past even the hysterical laugh. I was cackling and hacking, coughing a spear. Hopelessness cannot be justified by speech or by speech made relatable and actual. It comes out best in incoherent babble.

I fell, fading into the sheet. I fell, feeling gaffled. Baffling the time I spent crying out to the sunrise. Watching it climb instantaneously without measure over me. I battle with scorn. I am whipped by forces within. What an awesome onslaught; I'm so near the visuals; on the verge of greeting a hemorrhage (robbing Tom Waits again).

I used to be content balancing a diamond on a blade of grass in an attempt to bring the green back. Now, here, marooned in this condition, I'd gladly welcome an aneurysm. Despite this defeatist attitude I'm still pleading for deliverance. Stupefied as to why, or what deserves this.

My sudden existence has taken a turn. Scalding boils on my breastplate. Forces do find a way to penetrate. Substance drained a sunken mass wallows and weeps in pain.

xii

I see the sun has thoroughly broken through though I've never seen the sky so devoid of color. I am the dehydrated body, I have the arid epidermis. My garb is full cover. I am lost yet I feel confined in silence amongst the dunes. I don't want to go on without them. I refuse to move.

I endure the pain of the sun above me. I am pummeled by rank upon rank of its bombarding ambassadors of morning. This is real silence, without the sound of scuffing feet distorted to the extent they sound like brushes over a snare keeping beat. I never reckoned, and now I hardly believe: silence can stretch for miles and not even waiver. It has such capacity.

Distance is closing. Something is moving in. A sensational heightening of awareness fires like counter-measures. Some screeching steals my spell and startles me awake before fate can ring its bell and I'm serviced.

I'm alerted though still just a scab to pick off the land—lying there. I hear more sound; now more like human voices coming across the indicator board and loud, striking me like words pitched to my ear from a mound. Strange, what new motivation brings them around?

They whistle, I moan then yell out to these humans summoning me. The atmosphere has become sharply positive. They approach. It's them I'm sure of.

I have to know those voices. It's imperative to realize as well: we must be alone. We are out here beyond the perimeter—where there are supposed to be no stars. I'm pondering, they are moving in. I'm suspecting, discriminating. Initially everything is removed from objectivity. This area simply resembles a diorama; this is not a functioning scenery.

I'm confusing. I feel moved and want to get up and run to my friends but I am buried mid-stroke. Trying to crawl through these dunes. Can I be stoked?

I struggle to tread—begging. I've fallen sick here in my time without them. I've fallen into loathing my disparity. If only I could rotate, but for all human efforts I can't find an axis.

I'm so frustrated, so confused, so repelled by the graveness of the advance. I think I'll stop my journey for a while. Maybe I'll give up.

Slipping slowly—closing senses...
Setting into a dream...

xiii

Freshly lightened enticement disrupts the stillness of my lids; brings forth some form of a secret best kept. I imagined a serf, sitting in a wooden chair, up to a wooden table. I dreamt a pitcher on the table. The serf did not know if the pitcher was empty, full—half in either regard. It did not know how to regard the contents of that pathetically statuesque pitcher. Never found truth through the vision. No feeling of incentive beckoned. Serf sat there a still-life through countless thoughts hammered with the precision of breath and sentence.

Implore me; I am willing to release like gates. Nicer than taxes levied. Come in your own time, but don't be as the late Cobain. I give as much of the tune as you spare me; more sometimes out of absolute necessity but out of generosity as well. All the while actions fain dismissively I feel.

I streamed back into waking life. My friends dramatically recounted allowing my spasmodic body to exhaust. They watched on.

xiv

Feeling guided out of the dream. I questioned my fellows of our validity. Actually I just asked them how it sounded to head back. They accepted my proposal dubiously. I assumed we were all in accord. I hadn't the energy to delve into the past and our motives then react bitterly. I hadn't the energy to label and classify acts, or be afraid they were merely acting to appease. We were all in life together with vectors. I had no intention of undermining or prosecuting the mutual vision of end. I trusted evidence was prevalent enough to look back on in time, with a little of the right inside advice.

We were set on returning. We were verbally condemning distractions. My mind was conditioning theories anew; volleying verbals with my crew. This is enticing because perhaps in the lapse of consciousness I'd contracted a virus which proved to be catalyst to this unexplainable breakthrough.

It sustains only for a while. I apologize, I feel obliged to bring you down.

XV

The heat is exasperating. The sweltering sun, I wish I could curse it. Waking in drench my head felt like it was withering or folding, imploding, shriveling, or digesting itself. I had such a migraine. I'm frustrated because I silently known although we may be regressing. There is no guarantee. We'll likely not see the coast again.

I'm blaspheming and consequentially becoming rather bitter. We fucked up. We've taken this too far. We've been running on some impulsive sense of prerogative; *estamos jugando con el volante*. Have I had this skewed perspective all along?

Now too far to make it back our goals will remain unfulfilled and we will likely die in vain. I hate the residue of this matter but, what was I expected to do. God won't even speak to me, much less likely that for me he'll part the seas. We may need a vessel of some design. We document our attempts to further ourselves into the future, for the sake of plight, but first we must tend to the present, no matter how consuming it is of our time.

We continued it seemed, instigated by the rhythmic scuffing of three like pairs of feet. Not drawing any conclusions about our fatal predicament; lips too dry to make speech, throat too dry to swallow. I'm trying to gather up the saliva or bile from my stomach, just enough to lubricate.

The sun is pushing for the midday peak starting to shatter my right to appeal. I look to it for guidance because it seems like it could make me complete. My company and self thoroughly depleted. This heat is exhausting as it furthers its own growth. I see it in the way the light even with its distance is draining. A convincing quality, it occupies space. Sometimes I feel it is indecently.

A blinding glare generated furiously whisks wind up and around until it is howling. Trying to sustain my fixation I find fault in the blink. The light diminishes. Wind ripped dead in its path. There's the root of the star and faint; can't be too late in the day, only a few lapses to date.

Sun still is climbing higher, moving further along in orbit to attain the perfect vantage point. Actually I've been wrong. It is we who rotate on axis. The earth in fact dances about the sun, in a heliocentric fashion. We pass on by on our way around the round orb. This realization does nothing to ease my confusion it puts me in want to move past frustration. Certainly knowledge is capable of infuriating benefactors. I remain silent until the urge subsides and I am ready to renegotiate.

We very well could make ourselves some seats clasp hands and call to The Lizard King to guide us. Despite the irrationality, it is an inspiring suggestion however it was never negotiated instead neglected although for sake of, I did salvage my respect for his brashness. Still cannot embrace the whole without acknowledging Morrison's falling out.

The sun, the center of all attention gains leverage steadily. It does not deter, does not get tripped up. Why do I keep representing incorrectly? It is the earth with the steady velocity. Humans in motion even when in relative standstill; like utilizing an escalator or operating a vehicle. We are carried (and catered to) these days.

Under such mechanical consistency humans find trouble keeping pace, humans will succumb. That's the big difference machines are designed to overthrow. Humans best row, if you will. Although I forget how to, by now our progress is insignificant. I'm having a hard time keeping my feet in the steady progression.

Vibrating tones amplified break through the silence. The auditory hallucinations disturb me. Sometimes the dialogue is almost clear. Sometimes I direct lucidly. My head is merely an arena covered by dome housing. A theatre if you will—a forum at times.

I can taste the thickness of the reverberation as it finds room to linger in the back of my throat. I swallow chunks of mucilaginous debris. I monitor it creeping past my trachea and down my esophagus. Wind is passing through my holed out skeleton. My flesh by the solar blast was seared, and has fallen away. My thoroughly rotten marrow and holy bones provoke the passing breeze to flute through melodically. I'm a walking wind instrument; escorting the dead.

xvi

My brain is what it has irrevocably become: absolute mucus. Suddenly it's breaking the membrane and sliding out my nostrils. I lift my hands to catch snot and blood in my palms. I look up the desperately.

This is the blessing I wished to receive? That's irony, killing the scene. I tilt my head back and lose my footing, slamming onto my tailbone, receiving blunt treatment.

"Oh I'm so mad and man! Got to get you into my head...this filth is looking deep boys. I don't know who's most full of himself but I'm the weakest so you can float your temperance while I sneeze. Oh no wait strike that, got to get you back in my head."

"Fellows please collect me. I am in need. Am I pleasing you with paradoxical quandaries? Boxing this quelling tendency to be natural, what do you think? Possibly I am forming a clot. Possibly I can increase by repressing all I imagine. Stop the force of any rushing blood, this clotting blood could."

"Hey there, this seems like an adjustment in pressure—cooking my brain: textured feces, a worm cake. I'm defecating—no! I'm invigorated. You know, the sun has to rise by six, so all day we haven't covered any distance worth reporting. No, that's an improper use of the clause if p then q. It becomes an invalid statement but in time true—no, time as such a thing. You know, if and when we have dinner, it will be nourishing."

Lying back into the spot where'd I'd collapsed, lever joints involuntarily relinquishing; bloody caked nose, still running. I'm ranting while efforts are made to reinstate my constitution, to restore me to my feet. My body could not exercise control over my maneuvering abilities it was completely lax; they laid me back.

"Have your vision already," they finally remarked irritably. Stress has them clipping, nevertheless…

"…Maybe…okay…if it's time…"

I replied.

xvii

Once more inklings of interior control; the occupying light attracting again, this time nothing stops me, my eyelids melt to my brow and become non-functional.

"My name; that is my name," I announce.

A new crisp tongue is calling, **"Gortah, Gortah."** It's an apparition with hands, holding in them a satchel.

It's the man with the bag, now—what will he pull?

White light from the sun tinted yellow; intense ringing, I ask it to quiet in case I am missing all I am told. I am not frightened. I do not look away like I did before the apparition of my early youth.

There is no need to worry that I miss any information. The voice parts through the frequency. The man with the bag then pulled out...a tennis racket? Old with the tape on the handle loose from weakened adhesive bonds. Wrap, not sagging but noticeably worn. The frame appeared to be dented and played on. It appears to have been thrown in mounting frustration, in defeat.

He was spinning the racket around, sure in his grip of the handle. His soul was one with motion. He was not merely a machine that'd learned routine. He swung the racket. Lying there so near I thought he was nearly to tee off my head, correcting my momentary fault. The man with the bag said to me.

"Do you know this game, you start with love."

I sank, mesmerized by audible speech from this entity.

"Learn to play and lose keeping your initial quota. Love that, and then try to incorporate a volley."

Upon delivering this message and branding it in verbatim into my memory he proceeded to hit me with an instantaneous force.

I lapsed into the deepest imaginable absence. He left me to contemplate this transcendental expedition; for order to be exposed by method of expository.

The moral of this vehicle:

Learn to love and lose. Then when you lose, be comfortable with rejection. Just love that love with the love you can give. Love not to get on the scoreboard; not to conquer and have plentiful stocks of concubines.

Again

Learn to love and lose. Then when you lose don't respond in such a defeated manner with such frequency. You'll then know you are coming to grips and able to negotiate a volley.

And again

Learn to love and lose. Love for what you can give. Incidentally that will make assimilation an actual victory infinitely sweeter.

Until it's over. And again